*RIDE THE WIND*

A WESTERN NOVEL BY CLIFF  BONNER

*RIDE THE WIND* is a work of fiction. Names, characters, places, and incidents are either the product of the author's imagination or are used fictitiously. Any resemblance to actual persons, living or dead, events, or locales, is entirely coincidental.

Other works by Cliff Bonner:

*TOUGH CHOICES – A Dylan O'Connor mystery.*

## PART ONE: THE DEPARTURE

Everything has a beginning and an end.
Sometimes they occur at once,
The end becomes the beginning,
And the beginning the end.

# CHAPTER ONE

*"EVER RIDE A HORSE BEFORE, BOY?"* the stableman snarled. There was contempt in his voice, which I resented at once. It was not a proper way to treat a paying customer. And I saw no reason for him to assume that I didn't know how to ride a horse. The fact that I had never ridden one should not have any bearing on the fact of his rude assumptions. And *why* did every one in this town insist on calling me *boy?*

"Of course I have," I lied.

"Yes, of course you have," he lied. When I heard a couple of the stable boys snicker I wanted to run out the door, but something kept me from leaving. A cool sweat beaded on my forehead and ran down my face as I watched him ready a horse for me.

It appeared to me that the horse was rather too large for me, and when he put the saddle on its back I was fairly certain that I would be unable to lift my foot high enough to reach the stirrup.

"Don't you have a horse that is a bit shorter?" I inquired.

The vulgar man looked at me like I had made an awful insult of him. I freely admit that horrid insults about him had been dominating my thoughts, but asking for a shorter horse was not one of them.

When he had quite finished sneering at me he said, "You're a bit scrawny but you ain't short, boy. This horse be the right size for you if I say it is. And I say it is, so take it or leave it."

The arrogance of the man had gone too far this time. I am fit enough to choose the horse that best fits me, and man enough to demand it. I told him bluntly, "Fine, I'll take him," and wiped my brow. I wondered again how I was going to get my foot up to the stirrup.

Apparently the crude man had already figured that out for me. When he was finished putting the saddle and other tack on the beast he waved me over and cupped his hands together just below the stirrup. He said, "Put your foot in my hands and I'll give you a boost."

I felt a profound trepidation about such a maneuver but was unable to come up with a better idea so I followed his advice and stepped into his hand with my left foot.

"Now step on up and swing your right foot over while I lift up your foot a mite," he instructed.

As I stepped and swung he lifted, but it was more than just a 'mite'. I flew all the way over the horses back and flopped onto the ground on the opposite side like a sack o' grain. I laid there without moving while trying to catch my breath and gather my wits. I wasn't hurt bodily but my pride took an awful beating.

The guffaws of the two stable boys did nothing to lessen the assault on my manhood and I found myself fighting back tears. Thankfully my face was hidden in a pile of straw. I felt an unfamiliar rage building and something inside me changed. I rose off the ground and brushed the loose straw from my clothing. Putting my hat back on my head I turned and faced the stable bully.

Now let me stop this story right here for a minute and tell you an interesting fact. You see, the whole reason I was buying a horse at the stable was so I could leave town. And the whole reason I was leaving town was to get away. And what I was getting away from was an emotional condition that, these days, I would call a complete lack of sand. Or you might call it no guts. The condition had given me such a horrible reputation about town that I felt compelled to escape it by running, backing down from things being my ordinary way of dealing with difficulties, you see. So when I laid there in the straw crying and then felt that feeling of rage, well that was a first for me. I never felt rage before. Nor had I ever faced up to a bully.

When my eyes first met that stable man's, he was wearing one of those cat that just ate the canary grins. I continued to stare him in the eye and his grin faded away. Maybe he'd seen something in my eyes that scared him, but I doubt it. More likely he'd seen something in my face that made him pity me. He said, "Come on boy, don't get all riled. I just wanted to have a little fun is all." He shot a mean glance at the two laughing lads and it shut them up.

"You know who I am?" I demanded. I was mad as a hornet, yet shaking from fear.

"Yeah, I know who you are," he replied.

"Who?" I challenged. The stable man hesitated to answer."Go ahead," I challenged, "you're having your fun, now say it."

"Okay, I'll say it," he said angrily. "You're Milksop McGee. There, you happy now?"

"What's my first name?" I demanded loudly.

"Laddy," the stable man yelled in return.

"That's right, Laddy Milksop McGee. That's me. And how do you know me?" I fairly screamed.

"Everyone knows who you are," he replied in a raised voice.

"Yes, everyone knows who Milksop is. What's my real name?" I hollered again.

Softly this time the stabler said, "I don't know, son, I really don't know." He was looking at the ground and I couldn't read his eyes, so I couldn't tell his mood. Was he mocking me? Laughing at me? Or possibly hiding something from me?

I wanted to hit him. I wanted to beat him up. I wanted him to take the beating for everyone in the whole town who knew me only as Milksop. But I knew he would only whip me instead. And he knew it too.

"My name is Patrick. Just Patrick McGee. Nothing else. You got it now?"

"Yeah, I got it now. Are we done?" He looked back up and met my eyes again. There was no humor in them. He seemed eager to be done with it, which gave me a moment of guilt.

"We are unless you want to be paid for that horse," I managed, feeling that the money might lessen his contempt for me.

"Don't want no money," he told me offhandedly. "I'm makin a gift of him to ya."

"Why? You giving me pity? I don't want no ones pity in this excuse for a town," I said in an icy tone.

"Maybe some, to be honest with you. Hard not to feel sorry for a boy…..a person like you. But that ain't the real reason." I could have sworn that he looked a little ashamed.

"What's the real reason?" I asked him, unsure if I wanted to know.

"I know this sounds bad, but I been tryin to git rid of that there horse for a time now, and no one will buy him. I was hopin to dump him off on you cuz I knowed you couldn't fight me over it." He was looking at me defiantly when he said it, which confused me some.

"What's wrong with him?" I wanted to know.

"Seems he ain't always all that fond of havin folks on his back. And I *was* gonna make you pay for him. But now I ain't."

Feeling a bit riled up again I said, "I want another horse. I'd rather pay and get a good one."

"I know you *think* you want another horse," he replied, "but hold on a minute and let me tell you something else. There is another reason I'm givin him to you. When you come in here to buy a horse, I knew why you wanted one. And I knew you were headed out of town, on the run. You may not agree with this but I'm doin you a big favor by givin you that horse. He may be an ornery bucker but he's the best damn horse we got in this city, and where you're goin, you'll need him. Sure you may get bruised up a mite til you two work things out, but you'll be glad you got him once you do. It's the best I can do for you.....Patrick."

I was more than a little confused by now. First of all he was trying to ship off a no good bucking horse on me, then saying he wanted to help me, and now he called me by my real name. And all after he had just thrown me over the top of the horse as a gag. No one would blame me a bit for being distrustful of the man, but for some reason I was leaning toward liking the brute. And being not very confrontational, as the saying goes, I looked for the easy way out.

"OK, I will accept your generous gift." And God help me I thrust out my hand and made a shake with him on it. I think if I was telling this part of the story to someone I was trying to impress , I might get away with saying that I made the brave choice of buying the meanest cayuse they had in the city. I'd be lying of course, but I didn't know that at the time.

"Glad to do it Patrick. And before you go I'm gonna do you one more favor," he told me. I hesitated, squinting at him with a leery gaze.

"What's that?" I asked him.

"Ain't lettin you out of here until you can get up in that saddle on your own."

Well I might have been a sort of coward but I wasn't an idiot and I could see his point. What if the next time I needed to mount-up, there was no one around to help me? So I took up his challenge and walked up beside that horse, looking for a way to get on his back. I lifted my left foot toward the stirrup, but I just could not get my foot close enough to the damn thing. The lads were giggling again at the sight of me and I couldn't blame them.

"Think lad, use your head. You'll figure it out," the stabler suggested.

He was right of course, I had no choice but to think. I had no idea what to *do*. I stood there, looking at the saddle, and soon something about it didn't look right to me. After staring at it another minute I realized what was out of place about it. The stirrups were mighty close to the seat of the saddle. The stable man had been right earlier when he said I wasn't short, and my legs were a sight longer than those stirrups were hanging right now. It didn't take me long to work out the adjustment mechanisms and I lowered them several inches, which made them rather easy to step into.

I started thinking that my next problem might not work out so easy. That problem being how I would stay on the back of a bucking horse. I had never even been on the back of a calm horse, so, of course, riding a bucking bronco was a bit like running before you can crawl.

I reckon the stabler saw my hesitation. "Go ahead and climb up. I'll hold him. He don't buck long as someone holds him."

Why I trusted the man I don't know, but I stepped up in the stirrups and swung my leg over the saddle, certain that I would be thrown back down by the mean critter. But he didn't buck at all. He just stood there all calm and collected, and I sat that saddle as stiff as a steel bar, waiting for him to start jumping up and down like a dervish.

"I think he likes you," the stable man said, smiling. "Let's walk him around a bit here in the stable just to let him get used to you a little."

We walked around for several minutes and that horse seemed to care less that I was astride him. I started to feel relaxed and somewhat comfortable in the saddle. I didn't notice it at the time but I had quit sweating too.

"Okay mister, you're all set. You have a safe journey now. Where you headed?"

"West."

# CHAPTER TWO

*RILEY, THE STABLE MAN,* stared after Patrick as he rode off. When he heard the squeak of a stall door behind him, he turned to greet his good friend Shawn McGee, who'd been hiding in one of the horse stalls.

"Thanks, Riley, I appreciate it," Shawn greeted him. He put his arm around Riley's shoulders and handed him a fifty dollar gold piece.

"What's this for?"

"Someone has to pay for that horse you just gave away. That was the finest horse in the country. You'll go out of business if you keep givin horse flesh like that away," Shawn said.

"I owe you my life, by God I do, Shawn McGee, but there's no arguin your point now is there. You've convinced me how right you are, and that sure as you're an Irishman I would go out of business. So I'll keep the gold. Now come on, let us be good Irishmen and go to your saloon and get us a drink." He laughed good heartedly but neither of them moved. They both stared after the tiny object on the horizon that was Patrick McGee.

"Come on," Shawn told Riley after Patrick disappeared. "You're buyin the drinks this time."

"And why should I buy? You own the place," Riley wondered, truly puzzled by the concept.

"You got the gold piece, that's why. Now shut up and let's go."

They got seated at the pub and ordered a couple of pints. After whetting their whistles Riley asked, "How long were you in that stall?"

"Long enough, I heard everything. You were pretty hard on him."

"Not as hard as he'll get treated on the trail."

"No. Not nearly." Shawn frowned, his face worried.

"You done the right thing by not stopping him, Shawn," he said. "A man's got to find himself. He never would have done that if he stayed."

"Sure, if he lives long enough that is," Shawn muttered.

"And what kind of life is it if he kept sufferin the way he was? Might as well be dead if you ask me."

"You're right again, Riley," he said with a weak smile, "let's celebrate a little and have us a whiskey."

The barmaid brought the bottle of good Irish whiskey as requested but the usual grin on such an occasion did not this time appear on Shawn's face. He poured two shots and they raised their glasses. Both men drank the shots in one swallow and banged their glasses back down on the table. Shawn poured two more but didn't raise his glass again.

After a pensive moment he said, "I shouldn't have done it, Riley. I was a fool! I never took the time to think it through. The boy's as good as dead. I got to go and stop him!"

That he was some distressed was all too apparent. Naturally any parent might feel the same. But Riley didn't see it that way.

"Hold on, man," he said. "Have a wee bit of faith in the lad. I know he is your boy, and that you worry. And I know that we all think he is weak and a coward. But ask yourself, was he ever really given the chance to be a man?"

"What do you mean?" Shawn asked.

"What I mean is – and don't go takin no offense – but the boy was mollycoddled  growing up. He might as well have stayed in his mum's womb his whole life. Think how you might have turned out if you was raised the same way. You was raised in rough times and even rougher conditions. A drunkard for a pa and thugs and bullies for friends. Remember that time you was thrown in jail with a bunch of murderin thieves?"

"Yeah, so?"

" So you almost got kilt, that's what. And was you scared?"

"Yeah, so?"

"So your still alive ain't ya!" the frustrated Riley asked.

"Yeah, I'm still alive, so what's your point!" Shawn hollered back.

"I swear, Shawn, yur as tick heided as a Missouri mule. Do I have to slug you in the head and pound the sense into ya or what?" Riley was sure fire all riled up.

"Pound some sense into me? You an what army is goin to do ta pounden ya wee excuse for a man! And you talk about makin sense! Could ya just talk straight to the point and say whatever it is ya got ta say? You're worse than a woman I swear!"

"Oh, callin me a woman now are ye? We'll just see about that." Riley stood up from the table at the same time as Shawn and they looked as though they were commencin to beatin the tar out of each other. And sure they might have done it too if the bartender hadn't come along.

"Excuse me, Mr. McGee," The bartender said, "I mean, I know you're the boss and all, but…well…. the customers is leavin, and that means the money is leavin with them. And that means less money for me. So if you don't mind, sir, could you keep it down a mite?"

The two men stared at the bartender like a couple of village idiots with their mouths agape. And probably it was the mention of money leavin the establishment that brought a lick of sense back to both men. And at the same moment that they both became sane again they erupted into laughter and gave each other a bear hug.

"It's alright, folks," Shawn shouted out. "My friend and I were just havin a bit of a discussion. Nothin to worry about." Then he smiled and said, "The drinks are on me." Of course he could afford to say that now, after half the place emptied out, and the bartender's scowl let him know how he felt about it. As for Riley, he was happy because he still had his gold piece. All in one piece.

The two men sat back down, grinning ear to ear at each other. "Just like old times eh, Riley?"

"Yeah, those were the days. Look, I didn't mean to be beatin around the bush so. I was just hopin you would figure it out for yourself instead of havin to draw you a picture."

"I know that, Riley," Shawn said, "And I know the point you were tryin to make too. I was just refusin to look at it. Bein thick headed, like a Missouri mule I reckon. I was too scared for Patrick to face up to it."

"I know you were, Shawn. And thanks for admitten to bein mule headed. But don't go expectin me to admit to bein no woman now, will ya?"

Shawn laughed heartily, which made Riley feel a bit better. He raised the second shot of whiskey and said, "Here's to good friends."

Once again they drank and then banged their glasses down on the table at the same moment. Shawn went silent for a minute and he looked a little worried, but not quite as distraught as he was before.

"So what should I do, Riley? I can't just sit and wait day after day. It would put me to ruins."

"Give him a chance. He'll get tough, believe me. It was the tough life what made you a tougher man wasn't it?"

"I reckon," Shawn admitted.

"There's hope you know. He's already started gettin tougher. You didn't see the look in his eye when I threw him over that horse, but I did. He was mad, and for a second I seen some meanness in him. You ever see that in him before?"

"No, I never did. You sure about that?" Shawn asked, scarcely believing it to be true.

"I'm sure. And he figured out the saddle real quick too. He's a learner, Shawn. He'll learn to be tough. And did you see the way he rode out? First time on a horse and he never even fell off."

"Don't take much to stay on a calm horse," Shawn replied. "That reminds me, why'd you go tellin him that tall tale about the horse wantin to buck people off like that?"

"Just tryin to give him all the advantage I can that's all. What he needs most right now is a little confidence. If he believes that he is handling a mean horse successfully it will be a good boost for him"

Shawn grunted. "Makes sense," he agreed.

Both men were silent for a while after that. Riley watched Shawn during the silence and he determined that the man was not likely to stop worrying, and that if he didn't stop he would be likely to kill himself with it. Riley had to do something for him, and he came up with a plan.

"I got an idea, Shawn," he started. "Why don't you follow him for a few days. Kinda stay out of sight so he don't know you are there, but you can keep an eye on him. That way if he gets into any real trouble you can help him. Keep him from getting killed. But don't interfere unless it is life or death. Let him get beat up if he has to. Let him go hungry and cold and sore. Let him make all the mistakes he can. Just only get in the middle if he's about to die. What do you think?"

"I like it, Riley. I like it real well. Thanks for mentioning it."

"You're welcome."

# CHAPTER THREE

*WELL, I HADN'T GOTTEN ONE MILE* down the trail before gathering an accumulation of troubles. The most noticeable of which was a sore butt. This I blamed entirely on the rude stable man. Riley. His name seemed to have come to me of a sudden without knowing how I knew it. I wondered about it for some time and then recalled once when I was young and my father had introduced us. What was it he said to me? He said the man was a close friend of his. I immediately dismissed the fact as unlikely. My father would never associate closely with the likes of that man Riley. He must have said that out of politeness. The thought of that bothered me too. My father was rarely, if ever, polite. At least not in that sense.

I decided not to worry about it right now. I had more important things to worry about. Some of the rather large holes in my plan were becoming apparent. In fact it became painfully clear that I really did not have a plan as such. My only thought when I left town was to....well, to leave.

I told Riley I was going west, and now that I had that vague destination in mind I pondered some of the other nagging thoughts that arose. Firstly was how to satisfy the hollow feeling in my stomach. I was hungry. I'd been in too much of a hurry to leave to pack any grub for my trip and wondered now how people were supposed to eat on the trail. Surely there must be some inns along the way. I had money and could buy a meal and a room. OHHHHH! A meal and a room, how sweet the sound of that.

But I really didn't know anything about the country or towns west of my home city of Richmond. I'd never had to know about it, everything I needed was always to hand. Certainly I had heard talk about other towns, villages and cities. And the big cities like New York and Philadelphia, I could tell you all about them. The stories I'd heard of them were always so exciting that I paid close attention, and was always able to repeat them to others in order to impress them. But the small, the mundane, the boring towns, well I just couldn't be bothered to have a care.

I tried hard to recall which was the nearest town to the West of me and how far away it was but could not come up with an answer. Deciding that the next town couldn't be very far, I figured I would just ride until I came to it. Hopefully the town would have a stable because by the time we got there I wouldn't be the only one who was tired and hungry. My horse would need tending to as well.

Thinking about my horse was a reminder of what Riley had said about him being a buckin horse, and how I might get bruised up some until we worked things out. That reminder made me sort of pucker up and grab hold of that saddle with my cheeks so to speak. I guess I was afraid that me remembering it would remind the horse about it as well, and then he would suddenly remember to start buckin. But nothing happened and he just kept walking along pretty as you please, making me think he finally figured out who the boss of this partnership is.

This realization gave me a boost of confidence and I began to feel the thrill and exhilaration of freedom and the open trail. No more people laughing at me as I pass by. No more women fleeing the room when I enter. No more scowls on the face of my father as a reminder of what a complete failure I am. If it wasn't for the sharp pain in my ass I might have started singing, or whistling, or whatever it is that trail riders do to express their happiness. Instead I cussed that damn Riley again for giving me such a hard saddle. I hoped a town would come along soon.

No sooner than I began thinking of a town, I noticed something ahead of me in the trail. It was a man made structure. I was sure of that because it had the square features of sewn wood. At last, signs of civilization. As I approached, I noticed that the structure was a bridge. It was a short and narrow bridge across a small stream. I gazed across the bridge expecting to see a town but was disappointed when all I saw was more trail.

I rode over the bridge and kept going, anticipating the sight of a town any second. I hoped it would come in sight soon because every step of the horse was landing harder on the ground and paining my ass more and more. I came to a place in the trail where it was straight and level, and therefore visible for many miles ahead. There was no town in sight and I fell into a deep despair. I rode on, as if entranced. At some point the sound of splashing water brought me to my senses. I looked down and could see that we were crossing a stream. All I could think of was how good that cool water would feel on my sore butt.

I stopped the horse right there in the middle of the stream, climbed down off him, and immersed my arse in the cool stream. I must have sat there for a good thirty minutes, surveying the bank while my horse drank from the stream.

When I stood up out of the water I was mighty stiff. Every part of me seemed sore. I felt as though I had rode a hundred miles, but probably had only covered two or three. I moved slowly and with effort toward the grassy bank beneath the trees. The horse made his way ahead of me and started chomping on the nice grass.

I looked at all that nice shade and cool grass and thought what a great place it would be to lay down for a rest. No sooner had that pleasant thought come to me than it also occurred to me that I had no blanket or bed roll. But I reckoned that it didn't really matter because that grass was soft enough and, after all, I would soon be bunking down in roadside inns at nights.

I stretched out next to the stream, put my hat over my face and the next thing you knew I had drifted off into the comforts of my dream world.

# CHAPTER FOUR

*SHAWN WAS TRAILIN AFTER THAT SON* of his in such a rush that you would have thought someone had set his tail on fire. His horse raced along the trail raising a cloud of dust, more confused than a whore who set up camp in a ghost town. He was expecting to go to work any second but nothing arrived. No cattle showed up. No horse herd. Not even a hitchin post in sight, and he could not figure out what the hell all this running was about.

Patrick had a good hour head start on him, which he reckoned would put him several miles down the trail, and he figured to make up that distance before any foul deeds could befall his boy. He was so set on these facts that he almost ran right past him. Just as he was passing he caught sight of something on the bank of a stream. He looked back and saw Patrick, sleeping on the grassy bank.

He was stunned by the fact that Patrick had barely gotten a couple of miles down the trail, not the five or six that he had expected. He was also stunned by the fact that the idiot was asleep already. But mostly he was stunned that he barely got started on his secret mission and was already about to get caught. Patrick had to have heard his horse splash through the water as they passed and he began to stir.

Thinking fast, Shawn glanced around for some sort of cover. Off the trail to his right he saw a pile of large boulders high enough to conceal him and his horse. He rode fast and got around them before Patrick had a chance to look around. He staked his horse and climbed up one of the boulders to get a peek at Patrick.

The boy was still asleep, his horse was not secured and still had all of its tack on. Worse, he had slept through enough noise to wake up the dead and still did not have a clue that any one was in the neighborhood.

As he watched, Patrick finally awoke and rose up off the ground slowly and stiffly. He rubbed his ass, which was very likely sore as hell, as he walked toward his horse. He reached out to grab the reins and it shied away from him. The more he approached it the more it backed away. Eventually he made a desperate lunge for it hoping to grab the reins before the horse had a chance to shy. Only a tin-horn would try something like that. Any man who had spent any time at all around horses would know that you never chase after a loose horse. If you do they will take flight and run, and mister you would be afoot for some time trying to catch up with him.

That's exactly what happened when Patrick made that lunge for his mount. The old boy spooked and took to running. He ran in the direction he had just come from, back to the stable no doubt. Patrick hollered whoa! and kept on running after that horse like he really expected it to stop.

Shawn swung up in his saddle and took off through the brush. He was hoping to cut the wide curve that the trail made and beat that horse to the bend in the trail. It worked and he got there just as the horse was coming around. He knew he was only going to get one shot at stopping it because that horse was the fastest in the country, and if he didn't get a grab at the reins as it ran by he would never catch up to it again. He spurred his horse as fast as he could in the direction the other horse was running and as it caught up to him he barely matched speed with it then grabbed the reins, gradually bringing both horses to a stop.

Now that he had the horse he didn't know what to do with it. He knew that Patrick would come looking for it soon, so he had to make act quickly. He contemplated, briefly, letting the horse run all the way back to Richmond, causing Patrick to have to walk all the way back home. Then maybe he would change his mind about running away and stay there. He immediately decided against the idea, realizing that Riley was right, the boy had to go his own way.

He wrapped the reins of Patrick's horse around a branch on a nearby tree. Then, on a whim, he took a spare Colt .44 from his own saddlebags and put it in the saddle bags of Patrick's horse along with a box of bullets. He spotted some thick brush just off the trail that would conceal him and he hid in it just seconds before Patrick came into sight. He watched as Patrick limped around the bend and spotted his horse.

# CHAPTER FIVE

*"WHOA!" I HOLLERED, THEN, "WHOA!"* again, and again, as I ran behind that stupid horse, but he just ran off even faster. I was sure that WHOA was the correct command for a horse to stop, and when this one failed to obey I had even more reasons to hate Riley. My whole body ached, so I gave up running and just walked.

To say I was a little discouraged at this point would be some kind of an understatement to be sure. I'd played hell getting out of that rotten town of Richmond, and all I had to show for it so far was a sore backside and a runaway horse. Now here I was walking right back to the very town I tried so hard to leave. I couldn't help but think that I would be all the way back to the town before I caught up with that horse. I considered, briefly, going on west without him, but that was out of the question. Even I knew better than to try that. But the humiliation of showing up in town as the complete failure that everyone there expected me to be was too painful for me to contemplate.

Just as I was about to turn around and continue my journey west afoot, my horse came into sight. I scarcely believed my good fortune. It wasn't until I got close to him that I could see he had managed to get his reins caught up around a tree branch.

"Not as smart as you thought you were, are ya? Got yourself all wrapped up, didn't ya," I reprimanded him. "Well that will teach you not to run off on me again." I unhooked the reins from the tree and led him back onto the trail heading west.

Now, I admit I was glad to have him back, and even happier that he hadn't made it all the way back to town, but I still was in no mood to climb on his back. My backside was still paining me, so I walked, leading him down the trail on foot. I was about to tell him to come along when I realized that Riley had never told me the horses name.

I figured every horse had to have a name. I'd never heard of one that didn't. I couldn't go around calling him 'horse' all the time, so I guessed it was up to me to give him one. I considered several options, trying them on for size to see how they sounded. I tried "Blacky" first because the horse was mainly black in color, except for a couple of white feet and a small white spot on his forehead. It sounded okay but was a bit obvious and maybe not so original. Then I tried "Fury" and "Dusty", and "Pal" and "Pard", and many others that I didn't cotton to. Finally I came across one that seemed to suit me fine. It was "Wind", and in days to come I would find out just how well that name suited the horse.

"Come on, Wind, let's go find us a place to camp for the night," I told him. I already knew that there was no Inn nearby and it just was not in me to get back in the saddle. When we came back to the same stream we'd stopped at earlier, I figured it was as likely a spot as any to set up camp. Not that there was much setting up to be done. I had no camping provisions whatsoever, and no provisions of any other kind either.

Just because I never rode horses doesn't mean I knew absolutely nothing about them. I had been around them my whole life, and had known others who owned and rode horses, including my father. I had watched him handle the animals. And I had heard men talk about them plenty. After all, they are a prevalent part of life. So I knew that Wind's saddle should be removed for the night, which I did. I knew, of course, that a horse had to drink and eat, so I led him to the stream and let him drink. Then I led him to the grass on the banks and let him eat. Having learned my lesson earlier I kept hold of the reins this time. But it didn't take long for me to figure out that I had another problem to consider. If I wanted any sleep I was going to have to let go of him at some point.

I spent considerable time wondering how I was going to get shut of Wind long enough to rest up. If I tied him to a tree by the reins he wouldn't be able to eat or drink. And he might break the reins or slip out of the bridle. And it may not be good for him to keep that bit in his mouth all night. I had heard people mention these things about horses before, but today I had no other choice.

In fairness to Wind I held his reins and let him eat grass until I could not stay awake any longer. He would have to get by for the night on what grass and water he had eaten til now. I tied the reins to a tree and said, "Sorry, Wind. I know it ain't right, but right now it's all I can do. Please stick around til morning and I promise that tomorrow I will make it up to you. OK?"

I woke up around daybreak with a fright, panicked that I let Wind get away from me again. I looked around for him and to my relief he was still tied to the tree. He looked at me like he wished I would untie him in a hurry, which I did.

"Morning, Wind," I told him. "Let's get you a drink and some grass, okay?" I led him to the stream, where he drank, then to the banks where he ate grass. I took a drink at the stream myself, but I was mighty hungry and grass was just not going to cure my appetite.

After letting Wind eat a while I figured it was time for me to saddle up and move on. I lifted the saddle up to his back. It was heavier than I imagined it to be, but it could have been that I was still weak from yesterdays ride, and from not having any food.

Once I had the saddle on his back I attempted to fasten it, but I couldn't recall how it was done. I hadn't paid enough attention to that fact when I took it off. After studying the buckles and straps I eventually had it figured out. Once I had it strapped onto his back I stepped up in the stirrup and began to swing my right foot over the saddle. I hit the ground before I realized how I got there. I stood back up and looked at Wind to see what had happened. The saddle I had just attached to him had slid all the way around to his belly. Wind didn't like it none and he pranced around like his feet were on fire.

I tried to slide it back up on to Wind's back but it was no use. I couldn't get it to go and Wind didn't seem to like the effects of my efforts. So I undid the thing completely and started over. This time I pulled real hard on the cinch strap, sure I was cutting that poor horse in two. But he stood there for it like he expected it, and I figured it sure wouldn't slide around on me again, so I stepped up in the saddle. This time it stuck and I was ready to ride.

Next job was finding food. I was more hungry than I ever recalled being in my life.
Just the thought of food got me toying with the idea of going back home. At least I knew where home was, and that it wouldn't take me long to get there. On the other hand I had no idea how far it was to a town going west. For all I knew it could take me a week to get to an Inn, and by then I'd be starved to death.

Of course there were other options. I knew about people hunting game for food, and trapping and other such scavenging but I was ill prepared for it, even if I knew how to go about it, which I didn't. Home started sounding better and better, until I realized the treatment I would get if I returned. It was bad enough before I left, but if I returned a failure it would be unbearable. I'd rather starve.

We started west down the trail and all I could do was hope that we would encounter some sort of food before I died of starvation. Once, while riding along, I thought I heard a horse walking somewhere behind us. I turned in the saddle and thought I saw someone a ways back, but they disappeared so quickly I wasn't sure if I'd seen anything. I looked at the trail ahead of me again, and a few minutes later I turned back again to look behind me, but there was no one there. Maybe my starvation was causing me to see things.

It could have been a week later or maybe a few minutes, I was too hungry to be sure. But at some point I saw another rider approaching me in the trail ahead. Until then I hadn't considered what to do if I encountered anyone along the way. I'd heard stories about highway robbers and other types of outlaws and bad men. I always sort of thought that those stories were made up. Now I had to consider the possibility that they weren't. If the stories were true, and I was to run into one the bad men now, I would probably get robbed, or killed.

Wasn't much I could do about it at this point, whoever it was must have seen me by now and I didn't think I could outrun them, so I kept riding straight ahead. When I was close enough to make out who it was I was surprised to see that it was someone I knew. It was Brice Weldon. He was some sort of trader who bought and sold goods in the area. He had done some business with my pa and had come to our house for meals a couple of times. I didn't like him much. He was a bit slovenly in appearance and crude of manners, and he treated me contemptuously, which he had in common with most folks in town.

Brice seemed surprised when he recognized me. "Didn't know you rode a horse, Milksop," he said by way of a greeting, as we both stopped our mounts.

Well like I said, I didn't like the man much to start with and now I liked him a lot less.

"Name's Patrick, Mr. Weldon. Patrick McGee. And obliviously you are wrong about my horse riding because here I am riding one."

I didn't see a thing at all funny about what I had just said but apparently Brice seemed to find a lot of humor in it because he let out a hoot and began laughing like there was no tomorrow.

"Now that there was funny, boy. Since when did you become Patrick and not Milksop? Why, everyone calls you Milksop." He laughed again.

Brice was busy laughing at his own humor and didn't see me inch my horse up alongside his. And he never saw the back of my hand coming either, but come it did and it smashed hard across the side of his face. He quit laughing in a hurry then. He was stunned by the blow and it took him a few seconds to realize what had happened to him.

21

Even when he figured out that he'd been hit it didn't register right away that I had done it. He probably never figured I had it in me. When he finally did figure it out he didn't have much to say. He stared at me with wide eyes for a minute, then they turned mean looking. Guess he didn't like being hit like that.

I looked down at my hand after it stuck his face, trying to figure out how it happened. I had never struck another person before and the feelings I got from doing it were a confusion of thoughts and emotions. I didn't have too long to think about it, though, because while I was staring at my hand I felt a stunning blow to the side of my head and was knocked from my horse, hitting the dirt hard.

I looked up from the ground and saw the angry face of Brice Weldon looking down on me from atop his horse. As I was trying to gather myself he stepped down off his horse and came at me. I got to my feet just in time for his fist to hit me in the stomach. I wasn't expecting that and it knocked the wind out of me, sending me to my knees. Why I stood up again I don't know, but I did and it earned me a fist on the chin and down again I went.

I laid there on the ground for a second and felt that surge of rage building up, like it did yesterday when Riley threw me over Wind's back.

I jumped back up on my feet but this time I knew Brice would be coming at me and I was ready. I sidestepped just in time and his punch missed my head by a fraction. Then I ducked and avoided another one. He seemed a little rattled that he was missing his punches and it caused him to hesitate. In that second of hesitation I let swing with all my strength and hit him in his ample and soft belly. He lost his wind for such a long period that he finally had to sit down, and I was afraid he would never breathe again.

The idea that I may have killed him frightened me, but an instant later I heard him gasp a few times and get his breath back.

No more words were said and no more punches thrown. Brice got back on his horse and rode away. He never even looked at me, but I stared at him until he disappeared down the trail. I was still staring at the empty trail when I felt something nudge my arm. It was Wind.

"Thanks boy. Thanks for sticking by me and not running off." I rubbed his nose, which he seemed to like. And then everything went out of me and I knew I would have to sit down quick or I would fall down. I found a likely rock, led Wind over to it, and sat on it.

I had no strength left in me. I was weak from hunger, weak from the sudden surge brought on by the fight with Brice, weak from his blows and just plain weak. I sat on the rock a while hoping that a little rest was all I needed to regain some strength, and then maybe I could move on again.

While I sat I wondered about the fight I had just had. I had never fought with anyone in my life, and had avoided fights at any cost. The idea of getting hit had always frightened me. But now that I had been walloped a few times I was surprised that it wasn't really as bad as I had imagined it. After all I was still alive, and not too badly damaged. That's not to say it didn't hurt, it did. But I survived it and even tolerated it. And when I thought of that obnoxious Brice sitting on the ground gasping like a fish out of water it made me chuckle a little. The crude slob deserved it. Maybe now he would show people a little more respect.

# CHAPTER SIX

*SHAWN WAS AMAZED* by the stupidity he observed in his own son. To think that he really believed that his horse had actually gotten his reins around that branch by accident was unimaginable. Not that Patrick was a stupid person. He was not. He was a bright boy. It's just that he had not had much experience around horses, so maybe it wouldn't have seemed that far fetched to him that a horse could tie himself up. Shawn would have to give him the benefit of the doubt on that one.

He watched Patrick unwind the reins and lead his horse back down the trail. He didn't understand why he was leading the horse instead of riding it, but he had to give the boy credit for heading back West and not giving up.

He let Patrick walk on ahead for quite a ways before following. He didn't want to be seen and he could tell that Patrick was in no hurry to get back in the saddle so would be making slow progress. Eventually he began to follow him, and once again he almost came upon him in the same stream that he had just ridden past him in a little bit ago.

"For Christs sake, man," he swore to himself. "That creek is not the end of the damn world." He swung his horse around the same bunch of large rocks he used previously just in time to avoid detection from Patrick's glance around.

He used the cover of the rocks to watch Patrick. When he was sure that Patrick had not seen him he slid down  behind the rocks and sat on the ground. The boy was certainly persistent, he had to give him that. By now he had to be not only sore, but mighty hungry. Thinking about food caused him to recall some grub he had packed in his saddle bags and he pulled out some sourdough and jerky to chew on.

While some things about Patrick were amusing to him, others were surprising. He noticed that Patrick had seemed quite fond of his new horse and was taking care to treat him properly. Granted he was a little clumsy about it, but he managed nonetheless. Shawn even begrudged him a little admiration when he stood for hours hanging on to the reins to let his horse eat. It was obvious that he was dead tired, but he put his horses needs ahead of his own. He was learning.

When he saw that Patrick was traveling no further that night Shawn bedded down and went to sleep. Before dawn he was up and saddling his horse. He peeked over the rocks and saw that Patrick was already up, letting his horse drink and eat some more. Shawn took advantage of the extra time and ate a little more of his grub. He wished for a cup of coffee but he kept a cold camp in case Patrick might smell the smoke and come a lookin.

He watched as Patrick mounted up and laughed almost loud enough to be heard when he saw Patrick slide out of his saddle when the cinch slipped around. A short time later he nodded his silent approval when he saw him cinch it down tight the second time, and he had to admit that Riley was right, the boy was a learner. And he was showing some signs of toughness. Just the courage it took for him to keep going, and not give up, was a virtue Shawn had never noticed in Patrick before. Maybe Riley was right. Maybe Patrick just needed to be given the chance to become a man.

He followed behind them for a while, but once, when he got in a line of sight down the trail, Patrick turned in the saddle and looked back towards him. He hurried off the trail to hide himself but worried for a while that he had been discovered. He waited a while, expecting to see Patrick riding up to investigate. When enough time had gone by for even Patrick's slow gait to have brought him back, he reckoned he had gotten lucky and wasn't seen. He started down the trail again but was more careful to stay further back, out of sight.

After about twenty minutes of riding he saw a rider coming towards him on the trail. For a second he worried it might be Patrick and it gave him a fright. But right away he could tell that this person sat a horse different than Patrick. Soon after that he recognized the man as someone he knew. It was Brice Weldon.

When Brice got up close to him he saw a bit of blood coming from a split lip and the man seemed to be in a foul mood.

"Mornin, Brice," he greeted. "You okay?"

"I'll live," he said sourly.

"What happened to ya?" he wondered.

"That boy of yours sucker punched me, that's what," Brice replied. "If I was you I'd take some leather to his backside and teach him some manners."

Shawn felt like he might have just been sucker punched himself he was so stunned. Patrick striking another man?

"You positive you know what you are talking about here?" he asked Brice. "Some other fella didn't just knock you for a loop and now you're all scatterbrained or something?"

"He didn't hit me hard enough to scatter my brains. I'm sure who it was, although I understand your reluctance to believe it," he responded.

"I'm a bit more than reluctant," Shawn said, "I find it nearly impossible that he would, or could, do such a thing. What the hell could have set him off like that?"

"He didn't seem to like bein called Milksop, I suppose," Brice told him.

"What do you mean?" Shawn asked.

"I mean that he tried to insist that I call him Patrick and I thought he was joking so I laughed, and that's when he hit me. Wasn't a bad swing either," he said rubbing his cheek. "Kinda stunned me."

"Then what happened? Shawn asked.

After Brice related the story of his fight with Patrick, Shawn shook his head in amazement. He wished he could have seen it for himself, and felt a swelling of pride come on him that he had not felt before.

Shawn chuckled a little and said, "Well, Brice, what do you think you' ll be callin him now?"

Brice laughed and said, "I reckon I'll call him Patrick from now on."

"Reckon so," Shawn agreed. Then he added, "If it don't hurt your pride too much, Brice, you might want to consider telling that story around town when you get back."

Brice understood Shawn's meaning, and being a business man he responded, "And supposin I did, would we be doin some more tradin in the future?"

"I suppose we would, Brice. I suppose we would." They shook hands and rode off in separate directions, Shawn still shaking his head in wonder.

Shawn rode west on the trail for another ten miles, where he encountered the next town on the route. He was surprised that he had not overtaken Patrick along the way. He knew the boy was spent and starving and had wondered if he would make it all the way to town. But unless he got lost along the way he guessed he somehow managed to get there.

Shawn rode around to the back of the livery stable being careful not to accidentally run into Patrick. When he peeked into the stable he saw Patrick's black horse in there, unsaddled with a sack of grain hung over his nose. After he made sure Patrick was not in the stable he went inside, where he turned his own horse over to the stable boy and handed him a dollar.

"Any idea where the owner of the black might have gone?" he asked the stable boy.

The boy hesitated, it could be unhealthy to give out information to strangers. But his fear seemed to subside when he saw Shawn pull out another dollar. "Not sure exactly, but he said he was hungry and asked where he could get a meal. I pointed him over to Rosies."

Shawn made his way to Rosies and peeked in through the window. He saw Patrick right away. He was shoveling food into his mouth faster than he could swallow it, which made his cheeks swell up like a squirrel in the fall.

Shawn walked back into the livery stable and asked the boy if he could bunk down in the hay loft for the night. He was holding another dollar when he asked, so the boy had no objections. He climbed the ladder up to the loft and unrolled his blanket near the loft door so that he could keep a lookout.

## CHAPTER SEVEN

*THE ONLY THING THAT KEPT ME GOING*, after my fight with Brice, was the knowledge that if I didn't find some food soon, I might not live long enough to ever eat again. That, and I just refused to give up, because giving up would mean that the no-good people I had known back home, who held such a low opinion of me, would be proved right. It would prove to them that I was nothing but a total failure after all, and I was not about to give them that satisfaction – by God.

I rode on up the trail for what seemed like endless miles. More than once I was suddenly awakened while falling out of my saddle, and somehow grabbed hold of the saddle horn in time to haul my bones back up to the seat before hitting the ground. If Wind had an opinion on the matter of my riding style, he gave no sign of it.

I had, on occasion, experienced something in my past that I had described as 'starving' but brother it was nothing close to the hunger I was feeling now. I could swear that the skin on my stomach was getting mighty familiar with my backbone.

Some indeterminate time later I saw what looked like buildings ahead of me. I squinted and stared, and blinked and shook my head a few times to make certain I was not seeing things. Turned out that they were real. I saw a sign on one of them that read 'Centerville Livery'. I rode into the livery and fairly fell out of the saddle. I managed to get some money out of my clothes for the stable boy and asked him where I could eat. He pointed to a place across the street called Rosies and I wasted no time getting there.

I sat at an empty table and when the waiter approached I barely managed to get the word 'food' out of my mouth. He left, and several years later, but really only ten minutes probably, he set a plate in front of me. I didn't take the time to inspect what sort of food was on the plate, I just attacked it like the starving man that I was. I washed the entire meal down with a cold beer and then asked for more.

"You ought to wait a little bit," the waiter said, "You eat too much too fast and you could end up mighty sick. Might already be too late."

"Appreciate it but I'd like another plate now please."

"Your funeral."

The next thing I remember is waking up in a bed in an unfamiliar room. It was dark outside and a low-burning lamp cast cast a weak yellow light across the small room. I heard a rustling of clothes on my left and looked in that direction. The waiter from the restaurant was going through my clothes. I watched him take some money from the pocket of my coat, then turn around and look at me. He raised his hands slowly.

"I was only taking the room fee. I'm not a thief," he said.

"What's the room fee?"

"Two bits."

"Open your hands and show me what you got."

"Don't trust me?" the waiter asked me, smiling slightly. I could sense that he probably trusted me less than I did him.

"I have my reasons. Show me what you got."

The man opened his palm and it contained four bits.

"Thought you said it was two bits," I challenged.

"I did. For the room. You had two plates of food and a beer out front."

"I only recall eating one plate."

"I seen you was all done in and tried to talk you out of the second plate but you weren't havin any of my advice. You were passed out on the table when I brought it out and I couldn't find anyone else who wanted it, so you bought it." Fair enough, I thought.

"How'd I get in this bed?" I asked him.

"I had a couple of gents help me carry you in. Like I said, you was all done in."

Alright, he wasn't trying to rob me or he would be holding a lot more of my money. And he set me up in a room. Maybe he was okay. Maybe I could trust him. Either way it didn't matter because I was in no condition to do anything about anything. Truth was I was having trouble keeping my eyes open even now, and I didn't feel like I had enough strength to get out of bed if my life depended on it.

"Thanks, friend. Take another two bits out of my clothes and wake me up for breakfast." I was asleep before I finished the sentence.

Next morning I woke up just before sunrise. I don't think I've ever been up that early any other time in my life. It was quiet, and things seemed to be more clear to look at in the growing light. I kinda liked it. I sat up on the edge of the bed and swung my feet down to the floor. I grabbed my clothes from the back of a chair and was rewarded with a foul stench. I returned the offending garments to the chair back, catching a glimpse of myself in the small mirror by the pitcher and basin. I was a mess myself. Dirty face, greasy hair, and in bad need of a shave. And I stunk as bad as my clothes did.

There was a knock on my door. I wrapped a blanket around me and opened it. The waiter from the night before was standing there. I waved him into the room, wondering if he ever slept.

"I see you are up already. Coffees on and breakfast is ready. Eggs, biscuits, beans, hotcakes and bacon."

"Sounds delicious. I never had a chance to get your name."

"I'm Hardy. William Hardy. Most folks call me Cookie."

Having the bad experience with my own nickname I felt it was more respectful to use a mans proper handle so I said, "Well thanks, William. Thanks for all you've done for me. Can I ask you one more favor before I go to the dining area? I need a bath real bad."

"There's nothin you'd call a proper bath in this town but I'll send up a pitcher of hot water. Soon as you're ready come on out for coffee and a meal." He shut the door behind him and I heard him walking away on the wood floor.

A few minutes later a boy brought me a pitcher of water and I cleaned up the best I could. The malodorous clothing would have to remain in their condition for now. Clean shaven and barely less rank, I walked out into the main dining area, which was only half a dozen paces across the wood floor from my room.

There were not many people there. An older couple was eating at one table and a couple of men in nice suits were at another table. They all glanced at me briefly when they heard my steps on the wood floor, but didn't seem interested in me and turned back to their meals. I sat down and William brought out my coffee and food. I thanked him and reached into my pocket for some money.

"Don't need to pay for it. I found a buyer for your dinner last night, after I took your money. The stable boy took it over to a man who was sleeping in the loft at the livery."

"Great. Thanks, William."

"Do me a favor. If you don't want to call me Cookie, at least call me Bill. The folks around here may poke fun at me for the next year they hear you calling me William."

"Ok, Bill."

"Thanks. Now I have to go cook some more meals."

I wasn't as famished as I was the night before, but I had a healthy appetite and I did a thorough job of eating my breakfast. As I was finishing my coffee I noticed the stable boy from the livery come in. He asked Bill for a breakfast plate to take to his boarder. I was curious why the man didn't just walk over and eat in the inn, and asked Bill about it.

"Wondered the same thing myself, but a mans business is his own. I don't ask questions, especially of strangers. Could be a good way to find trouble. Already got enough trouble comes to me without askin for it," he explained.

Something he said didn't add up to me so I asked him, "Don't see how asking a few innocent questions can cause any trouble. How do you ever get to know a stranger, so that he's no stranger any more?"

"He wants to tell you something about himself he will volunteer it. If he ain't volunteerin, then maybe he don't want you to know," he said.

"Well, I still don't see the harm in asking. He wouldn't have to answer if he didn't want to," I reasoned.

By way of example Bill said to me, "Let's take you for example. You rode in here with a wore out horse, you was starvin and didn't have a lick of property on you. No bedroll, which is strange for someone on the trail. You had no weapons, another unusual thing. You got a bruise on your face, like you been slugged, and them clothes is not what you'd call ridin gear. Now, I'm guessin that you would get a might uncomfortable if I started askin you a bunch of questions about all that. Would I be right?"

I rubbed my bruised cheek while thinking about what he said. While I was thinking, Bill went to pour more coffee for some of his patrons.

When he came back to my table I said, "You might be right. I suppose there are some things I might be uncomfortable talking about. And I would appreciate you for not bringing the subject up. I think I see your point. But I'm not sure how it would cause *you* any particular trouble."

"In your case maybe not. But what if you was not such a nice feller. What if what you was runnin from – and I ain't sayin you're runnin – but what if you was runnin from something like a posse, or you was wanted dead or alive somewheres? And I started pokin around about your business. And you started thinking that I recognized you and I was going to maybe turn you in? What would you maybe do about it?"

"I think I see your point now."

He concluded by saying, "So if a gent wants to eat in a livery stable, ain't none of my business."

"Right," I agreed.

He changed the subject by asking, "You stickin around another night? Not that I'm pryin, just want to know if I should keep a room open."

"Much as I'd like to, I think I better move on," I answered. "Don't want that posse to catch up to me," I added hoping it would make me sound tough.

He must have seen through it because he said, "Sure, I seen your wanted poster over at the post office just yesterday. Says you're worth fifty cents, dead or alive."

I laughed at his joke and said, "That much eh? Makes me sound pretty bad."

"Good luck on the trail, mister," he said.

It was his use of the word mister that made me realize I had never told him my name. I guess he was practicing what he was preachin because he never had asked me who I was.

I stuck out my hand to his and said, "Thanks, name's Patrick McGee."

He shook my hand and asked, "Any relation to Shawn over in Richmond?"

I cringed a little at the question but sucked it up and said, "He's my father."

"Oh, I see," he said a bit sheepishly. It appeared my reputation had traveled at least this far west. If I was lucky it had gone no further.

"By the way," I added, "who is Rosie?"

"That's one of those questions that is better unasked." he replied.

"Right." I said.

# CHAPTER EIGHT

*I FELT  MUCH DIFFERENT TODAY* as I headed out of town. My ass was still sore but I wasn't hungry and I felt a little increase in confidence after making it through my first two days away from home.

I'd learned a lot in those first two days, and before I left town I stopped at the general store to get better outfitted for horse travel. I got a bed roll, a slicker, some cooking utensils and some clothes I'd be more comfortable riding in. I also got a canteen, some matches and a silk scarf for my face and neck when needed. I didn't have a pack horse so I was limited to what I could carry on Wind's back. I packed a small sack of grain for Wind and a small bit of grub for me, just in case we had to spend extra time between towns.

I walked to the livery in my new, clean smelling clothes. The livery man had Wind out front, already saddled up. I asked him about getting a better saddle, to save my ass more punishment, but he told me he'd never seen a better trail saddle than the one I already had, so I stuck with it. I remember thinking that it was a good thing I didn't have a worse one, or I might not have made it this far.

One thing puzzled me though. When I was packing some of my new outfit into my saddlebags I felt something in the bottom of one of them. I reached in and pulled out a pistol. There was even a box of bullets for it. It's origins were a mystery. I made some guesses about it but couldn't be certain. Could be that Riley put it there purposely. Or could be that the previous owner of the saddle accidentally left in in there and Riley didn't know about it. Could be a few other things but I wouldn't know for sure for some time to come.

I was not an expert with firearms of any kind and especially not a pistol. I had only fired one enough times to know I was no good at it. So if this new-found .44 was to do me any good at all I was going to have to practice with it. As much as I wished I would never need it, I was beginning to suspect it may become a valuable tool.

As I rode out of town the trail took a southerly turn, going mainly south by west. I didn't encounter many riders on the trail, but those that I did come across were polite and said their how you dos. Most tipped their hats and continued on without stopping. Those that did stop did not linger long. Many praised Wind and I began to feel proud of him and wondered if what Riley told me about him wasn't true after all.

One thing he was wrong about though, was that Wind was prone to bucking. Or at least he had never attempted it with me, so far.

After my meeting with Brice the day before, I was leery of seeing others who might know me from Richmond. I seemed, lately, to be acquiring a habit of becoming outraged by the same kind of treatment I somehow seemed to have tolerated for so long back home.

About mid day I stopped by a stream to let Wind drink and rest. I gave him a handful of grain and I ate a piece of the jerky I'd bought that morning. While I was stopped there, a couple of young fellas, about my age, came along and stopped to exchange pleasantries. They were dressed like farmers and had beards and wore strange looking hats with flat tops and flat brims. I had heard that there were some God fearing types that had settled to farming in the area and they had been described like these two looked.

Yesterday I might have asked them about their lives, but after hearing the advice of Bill Hardy I decided to let them volunteer whatever they might, or might not. They turned out to be the volunteering type and told me they were farmers and were returning from a trip to the nearby town. I inquired as to the distance to that town, wondering if I would make it there for a real supper tonight, or if I'd have to dine on jerky out on the trail. They informed me that it was only a few more hours ahead.

We said our goodbyes and I mounted up and rode on. The rest of the trip was uneventful until I was just outside the next town. That's where I ran into a couple of men who looked like cowboys but seemed intent on stopping me for some conversation. They asked a lot of questions that I didn't like and I was reminded, once again, of what Bill Hardy had told me that morning. I was getting a more clear picture of what he'd been trying to say.

These two gave no outward appearance of trouble, but I still had a bad feeling about them. And they were almighty interested in Wind. They seemed to take a little too much interest in him and I didn't like the feel of that neither. For the first time in a couple of days I noticed my face and hands were sweating.

I wanted to get shut of these two gents quickly so I told them I was hungry and anxious to get into town and rode away. They watched me go and I never did see which way they rode off.

I rode on into a town who's little wood sign said was Knightstown. I didn't see any knights roaming the village, but I did spot a livery stable , and I knew I better get Wind some good lodgings for the night before looking after my own needs. After all, Wind was my best, and possibly only real, asset. Without a good horse my chances of perishing became mighty good. After getting the gear off him I groomed him and stuck a grain bag over his nose. Then I made sure he was in a clean stall with a fresh water bucket, and I forked in a batch of hay for him.

Now it was my turn. The hotel, if it could be called that, was easy to spot directly across the street from the stable. In Richmond it would have been called something besides a hotel. Something not so becoming. But I figured if it had decent food and clean beds it was alright with me. Besides, there were no other establishments to choose from.

Unlike the last place I stayed, which was all on one level, this was a two story job. Eating and drinking on the main floor and sleeping upstairs. It was dinner hour and it had a good crowd going, but there was an empty spot and I took it. I ordered a cold beer and dinner. The fare was simple but prepared well and there was plenty of it. I ate a nice beefsteak, fried potatoes, beans and corn. They even brought me a piece of apple pie for desert. Man what a treat that was.

By the time I finished the pie I was feeling pretty tired. I asked about a room and a bath. They gave me a room upstairs and told me where the bath was. Since the last town didn't have a real bath, I was in good need of one by now, so I headed there first.

I suppose that the people in this town figured these were real baths but to me they seemed not much better than a horse trough. It was a temporary looking affair, more like a tent than a building. It had a dirt floor with some mats thrown on the ground next to the oak barrels they called tubs. But the water was clean and it was better than what I would get otherwise. I threw my saddle bags over a chair next to one of the tubs and got into some almost warm water and scrubbed up. After that I went over to a basin with a mirror and shaved. The basin was on the other side of the wood screen that hid the tub, and while I was shaving, my saddle bags were out of my sight.

It was a tin horn mistake I made, letting my bags out of my sight like that, and when I went to gather them up they were gone. I felt a sinking feeling in my stomach, and for a second I was too stunned to move. Most of my money was still in those bags. And my gun. Whoever took them was likely a far piece down the trail by now and I didn't know what to do.

I couldn't just stand there staring at the empty chair forever so I walked out into the street, hoping I might see someone carrying my bags. That'd be a long-shot but it was worth a try. I walked up the street from one end of town to the next. I looked in all the stores and saloons, of which there was only two. I checked the backs of any horses that were hitched up in the street. But I didn't see any sign of my bags.

I walked around to the back of all the buildings in case there was something to be found there, but there wasn't. I had seen a sheriffs' sign on one of the doors in the street so I walked back around and knocked on the door. It took a while for someone to answer and when they did they looked like they'd been sleeping.

The sheriff was an old man with gray hair and a big belly. He smelled of whiskey and I figured him out pretty quick as no one to trust for help. But just in case, I told him about my saddle bags. He never said a word, he just closed the door on me and I watched through the glass as he walked back to his bunk and lay down.

I went back to my hotel room. I sat on the bed and pondered my situation. I didn't like the thought at all, but I was starting to accept the idea that I could still make it without my bags, and money, and gun. Somehow. I laid back on the bed and sank deeper into my despair. Eventually I reached a point where I felt like crying, and it reminded me of how I felt when I was laying on the floor of the stable after Riley threw me over Wind's back. I felt the rage come on me and I was mad. I made up my mind to go back to the sheriff and wake him up and make him do something. Like his job.

I left my room and stalked down the stairs. I had almost made it out the door when something from the corner of my eye caught my attention. It was a pink silk.

Now, I mentioned earlier that I bought some new clothes back down the trail in the last town, and that one of them was a silk. But what I didn't say was that it was pink. I know what you're thinking but it was the only one they had, or so they said, and at the time I thought that the item was vital enough that I should get it no matter what color it was. For sure I had wondered if that pink silk wouldn't bring plenty of troubles down on me in my future, but tonight it was going to save my bacon. Or so I believed.

One of those cowboys who had stopped me outside of town was trying to give the pink silk to one of the girls in the saloon. He probably thought it would buy him some attention from the pretty young lady. Whether that was true or not I didn't know, but he had definitely gotten *my* attention.

One day I would learn to control my rage and turn it to something useful, but today was not the day. Under the influence of that rage I forged ahead, making more tin horn mistakes in the process. I went straight at the man, blind to anything else around me. And deaf too apparently, because the cowboy's partner saw me coming and gave a warning to his friend who turned and saw me coming at him. That took away any advantage of surprise and he was ready for me. I cocked my fist back intending a blow hard enough to separate his head from his shoulders, and it was the last thing I remembered before waking up in my room.

# CHAPTER NINE

*SHAWN FINISHED HIS BREAKFAST* in the Centerville stable loft and waited for Patrick to come get his horse. He had instructed the stable boy to have the black saddled and waiting out front of the stable for Patrick. That way he could avoid encountering Patrick, and reduce the chances that Patrick would see his own horse and recognize it.

He watched through a crack in the plank as Patrick loaded up his horse with a fairly good outfit. He'd learned alright. He was learning what was needed on the trail and Shawn admitted to himself that the boy had outfitted himself with most of the important things. And he smiled to himself when he saw Patrick discover the gun in his saddle bags.

Shawn was grateful, too, that Patrick had a pretty uneventful night last night. He had spent it eating and resting, which was smart. Shawn had given a dollar to both the innkeeper and the stable boy to alert him if there was any trouble. But his sleep was never interrupted by them, which allowed him to get some good rest himself.

Patrick was about an hour down the trail when Shawn finally rode out behind him. He followed for the entire day and was surprised that Patrick persisted in the saddle all the way to the next town. He had accomplished a good bit of riding that day.

Just as he was approaching Knightsville he saw two riders setting in the trail and looking towards town. Shawn followed their gaze and noticed that they were looking at Patrick as he rode into town.

He recognized the two cowboys for what they were; no goods. Their run down clothing and boots, and their slovenly appearance indicated that they were not prone to honest work nor hard labor. He had seen their type too often and they were usually bent on only one thing – trouble. He decided he better keep an eye on them.

He rode on by them and said howdy as he passed. They nodded in return but said nothing. He took careful notice of their guns as he rode by. They both had two pistols holstered at their hips, and the blond mean lookin one had a lever action rifle in a saddle scabbard. The tall dark faced man with pock marks carried a bowie type knife in his boot.

Instead of going directly to the stable, Shawn rode part way down the main street and then turned right, up an ally, where he found a small copse of cottonwoods just on the outskirts of town. He circled around them back to the trail he had just come in on and picked a spot where he could watch the two low life cowboys. He wasn't sure what they were up to, but he was sure they were up to something, and he wanted to see it when it happened.

The two no-accounts were still alongside the trail, but before long they rode towards town. They avoided the main road and rode around to the backside of the hotel and saloon.

Shawn circled around to where they had ridden but in the opposite direction. He stayed well back from them, taking cover in some bushes where he could watch. Their horses were tied up but the two men were not in sight, meaning they must be inside somewhere.

Leaving his horse tied to a tree he went on foot, trying to use any cover he could find as he went. He sat behind a large boulder that was only about thirty feet from the buildings. A little closer to him was a tent-like structure that he assumed was a make shift bath house. He had seen many like it before. He waited there for another hour and heard someone coming out of one of the buildings. Two men were talking just on the other side of the bath tent canvass wall.

One of them was a bit excited. He said, "Ok, he's comin out to have a bath, keep an eye out." A second later one of the no-accounts came into sight.

He watched the man for a good twenty minutes, while he waited for their victim to make a mistake which would put him at a disadvantage. Then pock face slipped into the bath tent through a slit in the canvas. A half minute later he came back out carrying a set of saddle bags, just as Blondie rode up on a horse. Pock face handed the saddle bags up to Blondie and for a second Shawn had a clear look at them. He recognized them at once as Patrick's. Pock face mounted his horse and the two rode off.

Shawn mounted up quickly and followed them.

They rode down into a shallow ravine where they wouldn't be seen and searched the contents of the stolen saddle bags. They transferred the contents into their own saddle bags and left the empty ones on the ground. Shawn was expecting them to ride swiftly off down the trail, far away from possible discovery and the justice of the law. He planned to ride them down and bring them to his own terms of justice, but they surprised him and rode back into town.

He rode into the ravine and picked up Patrick's emptied bags, then followed the thieves at a safe distance. When they approached the hotel he veered off and went up an ally. He tied up his horse and looked around the corner of the building, seeing the two men enter the saloon. He watched the street wondering what his next action should be. He was just about to step out into the street when he saw Patrick come out of the hotel. He ducked back behind the building to avoid discovery.

After waiting a moment he took another look down the street and saw Patrick walking to the other end of town. He was looking at all the horses and checking out the buildings. He got to the end of town and turned around, coming back towards Shawn. As he grew closer Shawn had to mount his horse and get out of the ally so he wouldn't be seen. He returned to the back of the buildings, back to his former hidey hole. He watched as Patrick went up and down the backs of the buildings, looking for his saddle bags no doubt.

When Patrick went back into his hotel, Shawn left his horse hidden in the bushes and walked around to the back door of the saloon. He cracked the door a little and peered inside. He saw the blond cowboy flirting with one of the barmaids. He was buying drinks for her and giving her plenty of attention. He was trying to tie a pink silk around her neck and steal a kiss while doing it. Pock face was seated near the entrance, alone at a table nursing a shot of rye. He watched the door and Shawn realized he was the half of the duo with at least part of a brain. Shawn watched them for a few minutes and then his attention was drawn to the front door where someone was coming inside. He saw that pock face had noticed the new arrival as well.

Patrick walked through that door with a look of rage on his face that Shawn had never seen before. It stunned Shawn and he froze, not knowing how to react. To his amazement Patrick walked right up to the blonde thief and cocked his fist as if to strike him. It was a noble and unprecedented gesture on his part, but his swing was painfully slow, and pock face had warned his friend by yelling, "Watch out, Zeke!"

Zeke turned just in time to see Patrick and before he could execute his swing the blonde thief hit him square on the jaw, and it was lights out for Patrick.

No longer frozen with surprise Shawn acted quickly. In one fluid motion he entered the room, drew his pistol and struck the blond dry gulcher on the back of the head with it. He went down in a heap and before he hit the floor Shawn had his gun pointed at his pock face partner, who had just reached for his own pistol. Seeing that he had

40

been too slow on the draw he wisely moved his hand away from the gun and raised both hands above his shoulders trying to avoid a sudden death.

At this point the sheriff walked in the front door. He looked sleepy and Shawn wondered what woke him. No shots were fired and they hadn't made enough noise to wake him up. He guessed that a bystander must have gone to his office and informed him of the trouble.

The sheriff sized up the situation quickly. Shawn had one man covered with his gun and the outlaw still had his hands in the air when the sheriff spoke.

"What happened here?" he asked, peering down at the two men on the floor. He must have recognized Patrick.

"Him again," he commented. "Humph."

"What do you mean by 'again'?" Shawn asked instead of explaining things to the sheriff.

"He came to my office tonight. Seems he left his saddle bags layin around and they got stoled." He looked over at pock face and said, "Put your hands down Ed. And hand me your gun. Slowly."

Ed complied and handed the sheriff his gun. "Looks like you two bought yourselves a passel of trouble this time," he said as he pocketed Ed's gun.

The sheriff turned to Shawn and said, "Put your gun away now. I won't have no more trouble here tonight."

"If you didn't want trouble then you should have come after these two dry gulchers yourself, when Patrick there asked for your help, and retrieved the saddle bags they stole. Instead you went to bed and left it in his hands to get them back." He pointed to Patrick on the floor. "And I had to help him, so now here we are."

"Alright, you got your bags back so now its over. Put your gun away," the sheriff replied.

"No. It ain't over yet. I want all of the contents returned to his saddle bags." He threw Patrick's bags on the bar. "And then I want them taken up to his room. Then I want him taken to his room and put on his bed. Then you lock these two up."

The sheriff seen a determined look in Shawn's eyes and knew there was no give in the man.

"Do it," he ordered Ed. "Put everything back. Now!"

Ed did what he was told. He put the money in the bags, then walked up to Zeke and took a gun out of the back of his belt and put that in the bags. "The rest of the stuff is in my outfit, on my horse out front."

The sheriff went out and came back with a set of saddle bags and handed them to Ed who transferred the rest of Patrick's things to his saddle bags. Then Ed walked over the the bar girl and took back the pink silk. He added it to the bags.

It irritated Shawn that Ed put that scarf in there. "What was that for?" he demanded.

"It was his. It was in the bags. You said put it all back, so I did," he said.

All three men exchanged questioning glances and Ed just shrugged.

"Now lock these two idiots up," Shawn said.

The sheriff looked at Ed and said, "You drag Zeke over to the jail and stay there. If you ain't there when I come back I'll find you and shoot you both. You hear?"

"Yeah," Ed said, then he walked over and grabbed Zeke by the boots and started dragging.

"Me and you will take this other one up to his room," the sheriff said to Shawn.

When they were done putting Patrick to bed they walked back to the saloon. On the walk back the sheriff asked, "Who are you, mister?"

"Shawn McGee, from Richmond."

"Heard of ya. I'm Brand. Brand Johnston." They shook hands.

Shawn had heard of him. He had a pretty good reputation as a lawman at one time. But like all men do, eventually he had gotten old and lost his edge. Now he was just hoping to spend his last years in a small town which had few troubles to deal with, and none of them serious if he was lucky.

That meant that Zeke and Ed must not have been real hard cases or Brand wouldn't let them hang around. And the fact that Ed had arrested both himself and his partner on Brand's command said something about them, and about Brand. He still had a presence, and his threats were still taken seriously. Sometimes a man's reputation can serve him for a long time, especially if he earned it honest like. But he had to be willing to back the reputation up with action if the need ever came.

"Who'd we just put to bed?" Brand wondered.

"My son, Patrick."

"Heard of him too. But they called him Milksop."

"Not no more they don't. Not no more," Shawn replied.

Brand nodded and said, "Whatever you say, mister."

Shawn told Brand about Patrick leaving Richmond of his own accord and about his trip so far. And he explained why he was following him. By then they had arrived back at the saloon and ordered a drink.

"So you see, Brand," Shawn said after the bartender poured their whiskeys, "I would appreciate it if Patrick never knew that I was here tonight."

"I'll see he doesn't. And I'll see he gets out of town safe. Now I got to go lock up those two no-accounts." They shook hands and Brand left the saloon to go back to his office.

Shawn finished his drink and retrieved his horse from where he had hidden it, then he took it to the stable and got him settled in. Once again he would not be able to stay at the inn so he bunked down in the livery loft.

## CHAPTER TEN

*I WAS AWAKE BUT I WASN'T MOVING.* I laid in bed and rubbed my jaw, which was damn sore. I tried moving my head to get a look around and it hurt every time I moved it. It took me a few minutes to remember where I was, and where I'd been. I'd gone after that thief that stole my saddle bags. And I did it like a mad bull. And look what it got me – just a beating, and none of my outfit returned. I made up my mind I was gonna have to get a handle on acting like that. I was tired of waking up in rooms without knowing how I got there.

I sat up in the bed slowly, intending to get some water on my face and try to wake up. I looked toward the water jug to gauge it's distance and my ability to cover it. I was startled to see my stolen saddle bags hanging over the back of the chair in front of the water basin. At first I thought I was seeing things as a result of having my brains knocked in. I closed my eyes for a minute, but when I opened them again the saddlebags were still there.

They were too far from the bed for me to reach out and get hold of them without standing up. So I took the couple of steps it took to reach them and then sat back down on the bed. I checked the contents and they were all there. Even the pink silk which I had seen the cowboy giving to the girl. It made no sense. How did it all get back in my room?

I didn't know exactly how long I'd been knocked out but it was still dark, and I was pretty sure I hadn't been out a whole day. Being too tired to ponder the mysteries of my saddle bags I laid back down in the bed and slept some more.

When I woke up again it was coming near daylight. In spite of a sore jaw I was ready to travel. After last night I figured the more distance I put between me and this town the better.

I put my boots on and grabbed my saddle bags, which got me thinking about their mysterious return again. I wondered if I would ever know what happened while I was knocked out. Whatever it was that happened, I made up my mind I wasn't going to take any more chances on losing my saddle bags, so I took the pistol out of them and checked to see if it was loaded. Satisfied that it was, I tucked it in my belt, promising to buy a holster for it.

I ambled over to the livery, happy to see Wind again. He nudged me and nickered like he was happy to see me too. Not sure if he'd had his morning feed yet I looked around for someone I could ask. There was no one around so I grabbed a brush and started brushing out his coat. A few minutes later the stable keeper walked in carrying a plate of breakfast food. He set it down on a bale of hay and said good morning.

"Morning," I said, "He get fed yet?" I asked, nodding toward Wind.

"Yep," he answered.

"Thanks. That your breakfast?" I nodded toward the plate of food.

"Nope. I got a boarder up in the loft," he said.

I figured it must be a common practice for folks to sleep in the barn along with their horses. So far I'd seen it done in both towns I been to. I wondered if there was a financial advantage.

"How much you charge to sleep here?" I asked the stabler after he came back down from the loft, where he'd delivered the meal.

"Usually nothin. But it's kinda understood that them that do stay will clean up their own stall and do their own feedin and groomin. Usually they slip me a large tip too."

I could quit wondering about the financial advantage, it was surely cheaper than an inn. I considered trying it in the next town, but I wanted to find out a bit more about it. And not from the stable man who obviously exaggerated the policy of tipping.

I took my time getting rigged up for the ride hoping that the man in the loft would come down and I could ask him some questions about it. When he didn't appear after many minutes I got antsy and asked the hostler about it.

"You reckon he's ever coming down from there?" I asked, indicating the loft.

The man shrugged but did not answer. I recalled, once again, the advice I'd gotten from Bill Hardy about not butting in to a man's affairs. I recognized that the stable man was practicing good sense by keeping quiet.

"Never mind," I said. "Ain't our business."

He shrugged again but smiled as well, as if he was glad that I wasn't going to put him into a difficult situation.

I got in my saddle but before I rode out I asked him, "How far to the next town west?" I was learning that information like this would help me make important plans that may save me from troubles, possibly fatal ones.

"That'd be Indianapolis, the last big town before St. Louis, and you might make it today if you ride real hard," he said.

"Thanks," I said, and then rode off.

Not more than a mile down the trail I was already imagining what the big city of Indianapolis was going to be like. I considered altering my plan of staying in a stable loft. I thought that maybe I'd put it off until the next small town I came to, and stay in a nice hotel tonight. A real hotel, not one of these glorified shacks they laughingly called hotels in these small country towns. A hotel with a real bath, with steamy hot water and fancy smelling soap.

I got so carried away with my imaginations of the City of Indianapolis that I got it fixed in my head that I better get there as fast as I could, in case it was further than the stabler said and I didn't make it there tonight. Or in case I got there too late and there were no rooms left in the hotels.

I put the heels to Wind to urge him on, but he was eager to go and didn't need much urging. He jumped straight into an even and smooth trot but I had to hold him back from breaking into a gallop. The boy really wanted to go.

After a couple of miles my hands were blistered from trying to keep him back and I let him have his head. He took off like a demon. I knew that if he could, he would take to the air and fly like an eagle. And me along with him.

I felt the exhilaration of having the wind in my face and the feel of sheer power under me. I lay on his neck and hung on, feeling his every muscle bulging as he strode. I had never experienced such a sensation as this. The close connection I felt to the raw strength of this beautiful animal was beyond anything I ever imagined.

I looked ahead up the trail, watching for rocks or holes or other obstructions. I could only hope that if there were any, I could somehow steer him around them. God knows there was no easy way of slowing him up. He was all charged up and his blood flowing hot and fast. Just like mine.

I wished we could run free like this forever but I knew he would tire eventually. A horse could not run this hard for long without floundering. He had already been at it longer than I thought a horse could last but I wished he could go twice as far again. He was breathing hard from the run but not struggling for breath yet.

The excitement of the ride carried me away and from some place inside me, that I could never define, laughter boiled up and out of my mouth. I hollered and hooted and laughed some more. The joy I was feeling brought tears to my eyes. Or perhaps it was the wind in my face. Or maybe both. Funny thing too, my jaw didn't hurt me at all.

"Go, Wind, go!" I shouted, and then I whooped like an Indian.

My excitement must have been inspiring and Wind broke into a new, and much faster gait that really stretched out. I stopped laughing and felt a sort of unprecedented intensity of awareness. Of necessity I realized that at this excessive speed I had better concentrate like I had never concentrated before in my life. I could ill afford to make the tiniest error in my motions or actions. My balance, my matched rhythm with the horse, my seat, the pressure of my feet in the stirrups, my awareness of the trail ahead must all be perfect or I would likely have a hell of a wreck.

I was breathing hard and getting tired, my leg muscles burning, but I didn't care. I never wanted to stop. Still watching the trail closely I saw a stream with a narrow wood bridge ahead. I wondered how Wind would deal with it. There was no possibility of me controlling him at this point, whatever he did was up to him. I figured he would just cross the bridge, probably in one stride length, but I was wrong.

From a mere two strides before reaching the bridge, Wind veered abruptly to the left and when he reached the near bank of the stream he lunged into a giant leap toward the far bank. I never imagined he could gain another ounce of speed, but somehow when he jumped he did just that, and I wasn't ready for it. I found myself bouncing on Wind's rump, looking at an empty saddle in front of me. I tried to prepare myself for the impending crash, but it is not possible to prepare for such an event. I knew I was done for.

Now, I know most folks don't hold to the notion that horses, or any animals, have much of an ability to think, like humans do. They don't analyze things and come up with their own conclusions and decisions about their lives. Most people think that animals just eat, drink and breed, but don't think. But after what happened next I am convinced that there is at least one animal that was capable of thinking.

When Wind hit that far bank I should have hit the ground so hard it would have left a crater. But Wind, bless him, sorta put on the brakes just enough that my momentum threw me right back in that saddle. I hit it hard and nearly flew forward off it onto his neck, but at that very second he sped up just a mite so that I would sit back enough to put me right back in rhythm. Then he just kept on running.

I have no idea how he kept going like he did, but after that near wreck I was ready to slow up. I drew back just a little on the reins so he would know I was wanting something from him. I increased the pressure a little at a time until I could feel that he was starting to think about slowing up. Then I let off a little. Then I pulled em up again, and I kept repeating the process of pulling the reins and letting loose, over and over again until he started slowing down. It took about a half mile but he finally came back into a trot. Then a few minutes later he was walking again, and I could swear he had a big smile on his face.

It took another quarter of a mile of walking for us both to catch our breath and calm our nerves. When I was near to being normal again I seemed to have realized several things. I realized, first, that Riley was right about Wind. He was a hell of a horse, and I could see now that if my adventure was to be at all successful I would need Wind. I also concluded that my irrational fear of horses had denied me the wonderful experience of riding for most of my life. Most important, I realized that I truly loved Wind.

At the next creek we stopped for a well earned break. I watered Wind and gave him a handful of grain, certain that he'd worked up an appetite. I chewed on some jerky and drank some water, then I sat down on a rock at the bank of the creek. I didn't bother to tie up Wind. I somehow knew he wouldn't be running off on me anymore, and I figured he appreciated the freedom of movement. When I was ready to set off again I approached him, and when I did he jerked his head up. For an instant I thought I was wrong for not tying him and feared he was getting ready to bolt. I stopped and didn't go any closer to him. Instead I just stood, and waited. After a few seconds he walked up to me and nuzzled my hands, looking for grain probably. I gave him another handful and then we set off down the trail again.

We didn't race down the trail this time, but neither did we dawdle. We kept a steady trot, or fast walk and sometimes a lope. We arrived in Indianapolis just before dark.

Wanting to take care of the most important thing first, which was Wind, I asked a passerby where the best stable in town was located. He gave me directions to a stable at the south end of town. "It may not be the fanciest place," he told me. "But it's the fairest and the most honest. And the feed is good."

He was right, it was a decent stable and I appreciated his advice. I paid for an extra ration of grain and a rubdown for him. When I left him he had the nose bag over his face and was chewing noisily. I told him I would see him in the morning and grabbed my saddle bags.

"Where would I find the best lodgings in town?" I asked the livery man.

"Depends," he said. "You looking just for the night or something regular?"

"Just for the night."

"Then you'd be wantin the Oriental Hotel over on Illinois Street. It's one street west then three more blocks north, right in downtown," he told me.

"Thanks," I said. I was eager to see a nice place for a change.

"Yur welcome. Hope yur rich." And with that he turned away with his rake and started cleaning out one of the stalls.

I skipped out of there all light-footed and anxious to partake of finer living arrangements for a change.

Thirty minutes later I was back at the stable. This time I wasn't all that light-footed and I sure wasn't skippin.

"Guess you ain't rich," the liveryman said when he saw me drag in.

"Not *that* rich," I said. "You'd think they wove the sheets on their beds with gold thread by the prices they was askin over there."

"Way I heard it was the pillows was filled with the down from the golden goose." I laughed and shook his hand introducing myself as Patrick McGee. He said his name was Trevor. He didn't offer a last name and I didn't ask.

"Ever heard of me?" I asked him.

"No, should I have?"

"No sir, you certainly shouldn't. I just wondered is all. Sometimes it's a small world and you never know." I was relieved that I was finally somewhere that no one knew Milksop McGee.

"You got a loft I can bunk in for the night, Trevor?" I asked.

"Sure thing. Ladder is over there. Pick you a spot anywhere you feel comfortable."

"Thanks. I'll look after the horse and his stall." I gave him two bits, then he went back to work and I untied my bedroll from Wind's saddle. I looked in on him and rubbed his nose a bit before going up to the loft. Silently I thanked him for taking care of me. He nickered for an acknowledgment.

## CHAPTER ELEVEN

*IT WAS WAY PAST DARK BY THE TIME* Shawn rode into Indianapolis and he was dog tired. He saw a person on horseback who looked like a local person and asked him for directions to the livery. He pointed him to the south end of town and he rode on in that direction. He was so tired he was only able to think of a soft pile of hay in the loft and curling up in his bedroll.

He found the stable and slid off his saddle, uncertain if his legs would hold him up. They hit the ground kind of rubbery but they held him. The liveryman came out and introduced himself as Trevor.

"I'm Shawn McGee," he said. "You got room in your loft for me. I'm dog tired and ready to hit the hay."

"Plenty of room," he replied. "Funny thing, I got another McGee up there already. Small world ain't it, mister?"

"Yeah, small world." He panicked for a minute and looked around to see if I could see any of the boarded horses. When Trevor wasn't looking he peeked into the stalls. There in one of them was Patrick's black horse.

He found Trevor and told him he had changed his mind. He lied and said he felt like a real room for a change and asked him where he could find a hotel. He got directions to the Oriental Hotel on Illinois St.

If he'd had any idea how far of a walk it was to the Oriental he would have tried to find something closer. His legs were about shot. Somehow he managed the distance and arrived at the hotel, still on his own two feet. He asked the clerk for a room and started to take a dollar out of his pocket. When he heard the clerk ask for twenty bucks he nearly choked.

"Got anything cheaper?" he asked.

"Nope, that's as low as it gets," the clerk answered with little friendliness.

"Any other place nearby? One with fair rates?" Shawn asked, making it clear what he thought of the Oriental's prices.

"The seedier hotels are on the other side of town. I'm sure you'll find what you're looking for there," the clerk told him with undisguised contempt for both Shawn and the 'seedier' hotels.

"You got a bar in this place?" Shawn asked.

"Past the stairs to the right." It was clear that the clerk didn't like Shawn and the feeling was mutual.

Shawn found the bar and ordered a whiskey – neat. He pondered the situation while he sipped his whiskey. Staying at the livery was out of the question. Of course, if he wasn't all done in he would have several other options to choose from, but he was just too wore out to consider them. No, he'd stay here tonight, but it would take most of the funds he had left, leaving just enough to get back to Richmond, if he chose to return.

He knew there were ways to get more funds quickly if he really wanted them. Funds that would allow him to continue following Patrick if he really wanted to. The real question was did he really want to.

He pondered on that for the duration of his first and second whiskey. It was during that second glass that it dawned on him how quickly Patrick had arrived to town. Shawn had ridden as hard as he could and yet Patrick had already been there long enough to settle in. That took some hard riding.

The more he thought about it the more he had to admit how much Patrick had already started changing in the past few days. He had learned a lot in a short time, and he was starting to show some sand. It was true that he needed help a couple of times, but he had taken some licks and yet he didn't give up. It was clear now that his mind was set on going down the trail, no matter how rough it got. Reluctantly Shawn made up his mind to let the boy go on ahead on his own. The thought of it still scared him, and he knew he would fret and sweat for plenty of days to come. But the boy was fighting the bit, and Shawn knew as well as anybody that the harder you pulled in on the reins, the harder a colt would fight em.

He finished his whiskey and walked back to the registration desk to speak to the unpleasant clerk. He thought how much the smug son of a bitch galled him, and how much he'd rather punch him than converse with the man, but he was just too damned played out.

"Here's twenty bucks," he said as he laid some bills down on the counter, "I better get the best room in the place for that."

"We only have one room left," the clerk responded, "But if you find it unsatisfactory I will be glad to give your money back and you can stay somewhere else."

"I bet you would," Shawn said. "Just give me the damn key." He suspected that there was more than one room available and that the little fop had lied to him. In fact he doubted that the dandy spoke much honest truth any time in his life, but he was in no shape to deal with the idiot right now.

He fell asleep so fast that when he woke up in the morning he hardly remembered laying down on the bed. It was still dark when he got up, a sliver of gray sky just beginning to appear in the east. He wanted to get going early just to make sure he didn't miss Patrick before he pulled out.

When he walked into the stable Patrick was there brushing his horse, who had a grain bag over his face. Patrick saw him come into the barn but didn't act surprised.

"Mornin, pa," he said.

"Mornin, Patrick," Shawn said, "How's the horse treatin you?"

"Wind is terrific. I'll have to thank Riley some day," Patrick said.

"I'll tell him for you if you want. I'm headed back home this morning," Shawn told him.

"Thanks, I'd appreciate it," Patrick said. "And while you're at it tell him he was right about the horse, he is the best. But he was wrong about him bucking."

"I will," Shawn said. "You don't seem surprised to see me here," he added.

"I was a little, when I first saw your horse in that stall over there. But I figured you had your reasons, and it ain't my business to know em," Patrick said.

"I was worried about you, so I followed you," Shawn admitted. "I guess I thought I should be protecting you or something. I wasn't tryin to interfere, I just wanted to keep you from getting killed is all."

"You didn't have no confidence in me did you? You thought I was a milksop, like everyone else." He said it mildly and without accusation.

Shawn cleared his throat and shuffled his feet and then said, "Yeah, well, I guess that's partly true, but you know I never called you milksop. I never liked that name and I never thought of you like that. But the truth is you had a mild upbringing, and I guess I never thought of you as exactly tough either. So when you struck out on your own like you done I guess I panicked."

Patrick cleared his throat and shuffled his feet just like his dad and said, "Yeah, well, I guess I know all about panic. It was panic that made me skeedadle out of town like I done. Heading out on my own

52

and roughing it like I've been doing is scary, but nothing is as terrifying to me as living another day as Milksop McGee. It felt the same to me as calling me a nothing. And if you're a nothing, well you might as well be dead."

"I understand that, son, and I'm going to keep on worrying about you because I'm your pa, but I respect your motives and I would do the same myself if I was in your boots. That's why I'm headin home and leavin you on you own. Just do me one favor," he said.

"What's that?" Patrick asked.

"Just post a letter to me every once in a while, just so I know you're still alive, OK? And if you have any idea where you might be able to pick up a letter from me just let me know and I will send you more money if you need it."

"Sure thing, Pa. And tell Riley thanks for the gun, I might need it," Patrick said.

"That weren't Riley, that was me. I slipped it in when I caught up your horse for ya," Shawn told him.

"When you what?" Patrick asked.

"Never mind," Shawn said. "Just do me another favor and don't try to use that gun too much until you practice with it a bunch, OK?"

"Ok," Patrick said. He didn't bother to say the he had already figured that part out.

"By the way," Shawn said. "I admire what you are doing, son. If I could, I would go along with you. But my yondering days are gone and I'm a business man now, chained to the work a day world."

"Thanks, Pa," Patrick said.

"You're welcome. You go enjoy your adventure, but don't forget this; Men, and women too sometimes, can be downright evil. And those that are, will not show you, or anyone else, the slightest consideration. They would just as well enjoy killing you as they would eating a fresh piece of apple pie, and would have equal remorse about either one. You'll know such a person when you encounter one. Trust your instincts to tell you, and then give them no quarter or you'll likely end up dead.

"My responsibility, as a father, is to protect you, and this is the strongest piece of advice I can give you for your protection. I cannot impress it on you strongly enough. Most men, like you, have good hearts and prefer to be peaceful like. To us, true evil is so unspeakable that our minds have a hard time accepting the existence of it in others. Even while your instincts are shouting out a warning about a truly bad person, your mind will start coming up with excuses as to why the person is okay. You might start hearin yourself say, 'he is okay, he just had a bad upbringing', or 'he'll be alright once the whiskey wears off ', and in the case of a woman it's always 'but she's just a woman'. All kinds of reasons not to listen to your instincts will pop up. But hear me son, if you listen to one thing I say, listen to this; ignore all those excuses, and if you can get away, run. If you can't run, don't wait, just lay em out without hesitation. Don't worry about fair play, because they would use that against you to kill ya. And never try to reason or talk your way out of it. Those type of people have some sort of deep flaw in their souls that no amount of reasoning can penetrate. They know only one thing; destruction, mayhem, belittling of others, and their only source of pleasure is seeing others suffer or die.

"I know how hard it is to accept that there are people in the world who only feel happiness at the expense of the misery of others. But don't doubt me about this, they do exist. And you are bound to encounter one or more where you are going. The reason for that is that where you are headed there is little or no law. Evil people feel a lot more free to act out their evil plans when there is no one around to oppose them or arrest them. You hear me, Patrick?" he demanded.

"I hear ya, pa," Patrick said. "But you make it sound so mean and horrible out there. Surely it can't be that bad." He was already feeling the very doubts that his dad was trying to warn him about.

"No, son, it is not all bad, and I'm sorry if I painted such a gloomy picture. The fact is that most of your trip will be filled with a lot of good. Fortunately bad people are a small percentage of the human race, even if they are capable of making the majority of the peoples lives uneasy. But when you run into one, don't dally and don't back down. If you can buck up and take a hard look into the eyes of evil you will forever know that what I am saying is true. It's unfortunate that for most humans, seeing and truly recognizing evil is the hardest thing for them to do. You be strong and face up to it when you have to and you'll be OK. What good people have on their side is that they are smarter and more able than a bad man. But that only helps once you face up to them and don't back down."

"Ok pa. I will remember that, and thanks." Patrick stuck out his hand and Shawn took it in his. Then he said, "Bye Pa," and got on his horse and rode out.

Shawn watched him ride off as he wiped a tear from his cheek.

# CHAPTER TWELVE

*LEAVIN PA LIKE I DID WAS BITTERSWEET* and I rode out of Indianapolis with all kinds of mixed up feelings. I was happy to see pa, but I was also annoyed that he had followed me without me knowing about it. I was annoyed with myself for not spotting him, but I was also annoyed that he didn't trust me to make out on my own. 'Course I can't rightly blame him for feeling that way.

And him telling me about those mean and nasty people in the world, and how I would probably meet up with some of them, kinda put a little more fear in me than I already had. I know he was trying to help and all, but then I started looking for a booger man behind every tree and rock. Still, I was determined to go on out west.

Before I left Indianapolis I spoke to one of the travelers who came through livery and asked him about the road west. I wanted to know what towns to expect and how far they were. I also wanted to know what the trail was like. The man I spoke to seemed familiar with most of what lay west up to St. Louis, but he said he hadn't traveled further west than that.

From the information I could gather from the gentleman I figured my next real destination was a place called Terry Oats. He said it was a French word but that he didn't know its meaning. I told him it sounded like a new sort of grain or something.

My next big stop after that would be St. Louis, and the man had told me that if I wanted to save some time and some wear on my horse I could continue on by train from Terry Oats. He said I wouldn't make it to Terry Oats today but that there were a couple of decent towns in between.

Wind made good time on the trail and we arrived in Terry Oats in a couple of days. I had no troubles along the way and no one tried to rob my saddle bags, or anything else. I had settled on riding the train from Terry Oats as suggested so I found the train station and bought a boxcar ticket for Wind and myself. We had a few hours to kill before the train departed so we walked around town.

I began to notice a great number of women on the streets who looked unlike any other women I had seen in towns in my life. Their gazes were overt and overly friendly, accompanied by a smile that denoted familiarity. I was not accustom to such treatment by women. And they dressed in a peculiar way, leaving more bare skinned exposed than I thought was legal. I figured they must be women of the night, of which I had heard stories from men I had known. But this was the first time I had seen them first hand. And these women were out in broad daylight. Maybe they should be called 'women of the day'.

I don't mind admitting that the women put a bit of fear in me and I tried to find a street where I could avoid them. That turned out to be more difficult than you would imagine. The town seemed to thrive on these women. Eventually we ended up back along the railroad tracks and headed back to the station, where we boarded our boxcar and waited safely inside for the train to leave. I was a bit relieved when I felt the train buck a little and begin to move.

The train ride gave us a chance to rest for a couple of days, and Wind and I both enjoyed it. I don't know about him but the rhythmic rockin and rollin of the train did a good job of lollin me into sleep and I welcomed the chance to be just plain lazy for a while.

Spending so many hours in a boxcar with only Wind as company gave me plenty of time to watch him, and I noticed that he was putting on some weight. I told him as much, but I don't think he liked it. A little bit later he turned a bit in the box car and dropped his horse droppings mighty close to my head. After that I moved my bed roll a little further away, and didn't say another word about his weight.

We made several stops to pick up or let off passengers but saw nothing too interesting. Next thing you know we were in St. Louis.

I could hear the hustle and bustle of the town before the train completely stopped, and when the doors opened I was surprised by the size of it and the amount of people I saw moving around. People of all sorts seemed to be rushing around on some important errand or another. Some on foot, some on horseback, some in wagons of various kinds, and even a few on bicycles. Bicycles were an uncommon sight to see and I must have stared at them for several minutes. I don't think Wind ever saw one before because when he first caught sight of one he shied and got wide eyed.

As soon as I was done ogling the bicycles I tried to take a broader look around town, but there were tall buildings which blocked my view beyond a few hundred yards. I swear they were the tallest things I had ever seen that wasn't a mountain. They must have been ten stories high, and I would soon discover that there were at least a hundred of them in the city.

We also saw giant factory buildings of some kind that had smoke coming out of tall chimneys. But the biggest miracle I witnessed was a gigantic bridge. Someone later told me that it was named Eads Bridge and was over a mile long and made from steel of all things. He said that the train uses it as well as wagons, and that when it was first built no one trusted it because it was so long and made from steel. So the builders of the bridge had to walk a bunch of elephants across it to prove it was safe. It was a hundred feet in the air, above a river so wide it looked more like a great lake.

After taking in the amazing sights for hours I decided to find a place for Wind to rest up and get some feed. I began asking strangers where I could find the livery stable and finally got directions from a man who looked like a real frontiersman. I had learned my lesson about buttin into a mans business, but this time I took a chance and asked the man what it was that he did. Lucky for me he seemed happy to tell me all about himself. In fact he had a pretty high idea of himself, but he was nice enough.

Turns out my impression of him was right and he said he was in the business of leading settlers on the trail west, to the frontier. So I asked him a lot of greenhorn types of questions about the frontier, and western routes and lands. He told me I was in the right place if I was headed west. St. Louis was known as the gateway to the West and was the main jumping off place for folks headed that way.

He explained several possible routes to me, telling me where they led and what each was like. He told me quite a bit about Dodge City and it's surrounding area. After hearing about it, I decided that was where I wanted to go, and told him so. He warned me about it, saying that it was a land of good opportunity, but that it was also filled with rough men, some of them plum mean and deadly to be around. That was the second time I was warned about evil men, the first time being when pa had done it, and I started to think I should pay close attention to the fact.

He also warned me about the land and the weather, which he said was more of a threat to a man's survival than any bad guy could be.

We finished talking and I thanked the man. He said maybe he would see me somewhere down the trail and I said I hoped so. Then he stuck out his hand for a shake and said, "My name is Jacob Snow, and it's been a pleasure."

I shook his hand and said, "I'm Patrick McGee, and the pleasure is mine."

We parted company and Wind and I headed for the livery. Once there I got Wind settled in, and then went back out on the streets to find myself some food. While I was walking along looking for a likely place to eat, I noticed a gent who seemed to be following along behind me. I remembered seeing him when I was talking to Jacob Snow and thought the coincidence was suspicious. I kept walking and after a few minutes the man approached me.

He was dressed funny. From a distance it looked like he was wearing fancy clothes, but up close they were thread-bare in places and a little dirtier than a fancy gentleman would allow. His boots were low heeled and scuffed up, and he smelled of likker.

"Seen you talkin to that train leader, Snow," he said to me without a greeting.

My old habit, of avoiding a difficult situation by running, started me walking in a direction away from the man, but he kept pace with me and continued speaking.

"Not too friendly are you?" he said.

I recalled again what Bill Hardy told me about buttin in to a man's affairs, and right now I didn't like it one bit how this man was buttin into mine.

"I just like to keep to myself mister," I said. I didn't slow my pace any, I just kept walking.

If he heard me he gave no indication of it. Instead he said, "Overheard you saying you wanted to go west. I can help you, and it won't cost as much as Snow charges."

I kept walking without answering. Jacob Snow had gotten me spooked about evil men again just before this guy showed up, and I was chewing real hard on whether he might be one of them. My first reaction to him had been a bit of fear, but my first instinct about him was that he wasn't too dangerous. And now I had figured out that he was just a con man. That was one thing I had experience with back in Richmond, and I recognized it here, so I stopped walking.

"What's your offer?" I asked in a gruff tone that surprised me. It didn't seem to surprise him though, he must be used to people bein rough on him.

"How much did Snow want?" he asked.

"That's not fair," I told him. "You tell me what your regular charge is and then I'll tell you if you are any better than Snow." I was setting him up and I was surprised to find it amusing to me.

He hesitated at that response and looked at me like he was trying to decide if it was worth messing with me or not. It was a look that I was used to giving others but had never gotten myself, and I got a little puffed up about it.

He was desperate for money because he gave me an offer. "Cost you twenty five dollars plus food and a ridin horse."

I was ready to drop my little trick on him so I said, "Snow wasn't charging me anything. So I guess your bid is too high. See you later." With that I spun around and went back to walking down the road. With a grin on my face.

I could tell he froze there in his tracks for a minute because I didn't hear footsteps behind me. But soon I heard him approaching again, and I had planned another clever response for him once he caught up. But he had different plans and I felt the sharp point of a knife in my back as he said, "Ok smart ass, hand over your money or I'll gut you."

I knew he was just desperate for money and not really an evil doer like the kind pa was telling me about, but still, when a man has a knife on you and is makin a threat, it can put a little terror in your gut. My next move was made strictly out of my own fear and desperation, and not any particular ability or clever planning on my part.

Without hesitation I spun around to face him and as part of that same move I swung my left hand wildly and backhanded him across the jaw. He went down in a heap and his knife skidded across the bricks . I kept one eye on him while I walked over to retrieve the knife so he couldn't get his hands back on it. What I found wasn't a knife though, it was a quill pen, like the kind you would sign a hotel register with. He probably stole it from some unfortunate hotel desk clerk. He should have taken the pen knife that went with it.

Holding the quill I looked down at him layin face down in the street. He looked up at me and it seemed he was about ready to cry. Seeing him like that was like seeing myself when I was layin in the straw after bein thrown over Wind by Riley. I had wanted to cry then, and if I looked anywhere near as pathetic as this guy did now, I must have been a mighty sorry sight. But in spite of my gutless condition there had been those who still cared enough about me to give me a chance, and even a helping hand. Without that I probably would never have gotten as far as I had.

"You okay?" I asked him.

"What do you care, leave me alone," he said.

"What's your name?" I asked.

"What do you care?" he repeated.

Passersby looked at him with some disgust and I felt embarrassed for him.

"Get up," I told him.

"Go to hell," was the response I got for my pity.

I never have figured out, to this day, why I did it, but at that point I laid down on the ground next to him and put my hands behind my head so it wouldn't hit the dirt.

He turned to look at me for a second with wide eyes before jumping up.

"Get up," he told me with desperation in his voice.

"Go to hell," I responded.

He was confused now and I could see all the question marks swirling around in his head. After a brief hesitation he shrugged and laid back down next to me. He looked over at me and we both snorted a brief laugh. That snort must have broke something loose in us because we commenced to laughing real hard after that, and you should have seen the looks on the faces of the passersby then.

When we finished laughing we stood up and dusted ourselves off.

"I'm Patrick McGee," I said and reached out my hand.

"Cal Jenkins," he said, and shook my hand.

"You hungry, Cal?" I asked, recalling my original intentions of finding a place to eat.

I started walking on ahead again, and he followed with me.

"Starved," he admitted. After a few steps he stopped walking and stared after me. I took a few more steps and stopped as well.

"I ain't got no money," he said dejectedly.

"Yeah, I gathered that, but I'm buyin this time so let's keep walkin before we both starve," I told him. He shrugged and we started walkin again.

"I'm thirsty too," he volunteered after we'd covered a dozen or so yards. I knew he wasn't talking about a drink of water.

"From the smell of you," I said, "You drank enough already. But whether you drink or not is your business," I continued, "just don't expect me to be buying you a drink."

"Yeah, okay." He said.

He directed me to a small dining establishment with a modest sign on the window that said 'Home Cooked Meals'. That sounded mighty fine to me and we entered, looking for a couple of open seats at the table.

Out of plain old luck we were just in time for the meal and when they brought it out the smell of it got my mouth watering. But it was the wonderful taste of it that made me moan with pleasure at every bite. Cal on the other hand only made the slopping sounds that a man makes when he hasn't eaten in a long time.

When we walked out of there, well satisfied, we stood in the street looking in one direction and then the other as if trying to decide which way to go.

# CHAPTER THIRTEEN

*WHEN SHAWN ARRIVED BACK IN* Richmond he went straight to his tavern. He didn't stop at the livery to see Riley, or stop anywhere else for that matter. When he entered his tavern he walked to a table without greeting a single soul in the place. He never spoke a word, even when the barmaid came over to get his order. When she asked what he wanted he merely put some money down and then pointed at the table, as if indicating where to place the bottle. The barmaid brought him a bottle and a glass, and set them in the exact spot he had pointed to. He opened the bottle and poured a drink without saying a word to her, not even a thank you.

Shawn sat in his saloon an entire day without speaking. His method of communication consisted only of hand signals and other gestures. He was singularly introspected, and even seemed to drink without any attention to it. Once, when Riley came in to get the news about Patrick, Shawn merely glanced at him and then waved him out with a wave of his hand. Riley recognized Shawn's mood and knew it was best to leave him alone, so he walked back out of the bar.

The town was experiencing a recent succession of exciting events. First it had been set abuzz from the news of Patrick turning crazy mean and beatin the tar out of Brice. And now Shawn had returned to town in a foul mood that seemed to portend something terrible. Shawn had not yet shared what had happened, but that didn't stop the town from coming up with all sorts of speculation about exactly what had transpired.

At closing time Shawn left his saloon and went home, without saying a word. Riley watched him through a crack in the livery door, wanting to make sure he made it home. He worried about Shawn, but he worried about Patrick more. He'd seen Shawn like this twice before. Once when his wife died, and once when he was young and his ma died. He came out of it quickly both times and Riley knew he would again. But now he worried that his sullenness was caused by another death, and suspected it might be Patrick. He hated not knowing, but he had no choice but to wait until Shawn was willing to speak about it.

As Riley predicted, Shawn was much improved by the next day and he came to the livery to see Riley. Riley, knowing better, didn't say anything but waited for Shawn to speak in his own good time.

When Shawn finally spoke Riley was prepared for the worst. But he wasn't prepared at all for what he heard.

"Patrick killed a man just this side of Terre Haute," Shawn started. "Killed him with his bare hands. I saw the whole thing and I still can't believe it. Figured if he could do that then he didn't need me watching over him no more, so I came home."

Riley stared in disbelief with his jaw hanging down. Shawn stared at the floor, unable to look Riley in the eye. After a couple of minutes Riley manged to ask him, "Who was it that he killed?"

"No idea," Shawn said. "I was tryin not to be seen and was watching him from a distance. A man come up behind him and tried to pistol whip Patrick from behind, but Patrick musta heard something because he turned quick as a cat. I've never seen anyone move that quick. He swung around and landed a blow square on the fellows jaw while his hand was still in mid air holdin his pistol. It stunned the would-be thug and then Patrick moved in on him and kept swingin until the fellow was still. Then he just walked away calm as you please." Shawn shook his head back and forth like he still couldn't believe that what he was sayin was true.

"My God," was all Riley could say.

"Yeah, my God," Shawn agreed, still shaking his head.

"You sure the fellow died? He wasn't just knocked unconscious?" Riley asked.

"I waited until they drug him off to the undertaker, so yeah, I'm sure," Shawn said. "My son is an outlaw now, not much I can do for him. God help him," Shawn said after another moment of silence.

"My Lord," Riley said, astounded. "Was it true that he beat tar out of Brice too?'

"Yep, he done that too," Shawn said with wonderment.

Like in all small towns, the story of Patrick's foul deed spread throughout the town like wildfire, and just like that, he was transformed from Milksop to a murderin outlaw.

It would be some time before Shawn told Riley the truth about how he made up his story on his ride back to Richmond after leaving Patrick. Riley didn't take it well.

PART TWO: THE JUMP OFF

There are rarely too many rivers to cross.
But there is always one that matters.

Doc Bonner

# CHAPTER FOURTEEN

*"HOW'D YOU GET US INTO THIS MESS, CAL?"* I demanded.

"Hah! Me? Was you that suggested we had to ride on a river barge," he came back.

"Thought you were the expert guide, why didn't you stop me?" I asked.

How we even managed a conversation was a mystery. It seemed it was all we could do to keep our horses from spilling over off the edge of the flimsy raft. The poor beasts became terrified shortly after the raft left shore and were rearin and snortin and jerkin back on their leads.

Wind seemed to take it slightly better than General Lee – the unlikely name of Cal's horse – but when the General reared up against Wind he didn't like it at all and backed himself right off into the river. The General, not wanting to be left behind apparently, jumped in after him. I looked over at Cal and we both shrugged and jumped in after them.

It was then that I found out horses were good swimmers. In fact it was Cal that probably saved my life when he told me to grab the saddle horn and let the horse swim us out. I would probably have been unable to make it to shore otherwise. We did make it to shore, thanks to the horses. Only problem was it was on the same side of the river that we started on, just a couple of days east of Wichita. Not too far from Jefferson City.

We'd gotten as far as Jefferson City, the Missouri state capital, without much incident. It was our plan, when we finally got around to leaving St. Louis, to visit the state capital because it was the only city created to be a capital of a state and was named after Thomas Jefferson while he was still alive.

We had plenty of time to make plans for traveling west because we stayed in St. Louis for three months, working. I'd pretty much decided to take Cal along with me while we were eating that first meal that I bought for him in St. Louis. Don't ask me why I did cause I'm not sure I know the whole reason. What I do know is that he reminded me of myself in many ways. Only trouble was that Cal was broke and I would soon be broke as well with two of us to pay for. On top of that Cal needed a horse and an outfit.

After a lot of threats and browbeating I finally got to him to at least consider getting a regular paying job. God knows in a city as big and booming as St. Louis it wasn't hard to find work. The problem was more a matter of Cal's willingness and desire to work. And he wouldn't budge off his lazy attitude til I told him that whatever job he did I would do the same. I didn't mind makin the threat because I needed the money as much as he did. Well maybe not quite as much, but I for sure needed more of it and I was reluctant to ask pa for it.

So we finally both took a job at one of the breweries. There were a few to choose from and it seemed that the folks here about took beer drinking to a whole new level of importance. Truth be told I rather enjoyed working there. It was darn clean in those places and it had a smell a lot like the feed room in a livery. I always did like the smell of grain.

I had hoped we would be able to drink free beer as well, but that wasn't to be the case. I reckon the owners of the place figured there would be no beer left to sell if the workers were allowed first crack at it. On top of that we worked in the section that didn't even make beer. It made something called King Cola, which was very sweet and had no alcohol in it. Mr. Bush, who owned the place, surely had some peculiar ideas about beverages. Myself, I would rather stick to beer.

Anyways, we worked as many shifts as possible and only took time off to sleep. We slept in the livery which was as cheap a place as we could find, and we saved up until we figured we had a good enough poke to take us a good ways west. Then we went out and found a good horse for Cal and got him outfitted for trail travel.

Like I said, our first goal was to see Jefferson City, so we rode out of St. Louis along the south bank of the Missouri River. We followed the Missouri west until we got to Jefferson City and then took the short tour of the town, which was only a few minutes, so we decided to take the long version. The long version was about exactly as long as the short one. But we enjoyed it and then headed out on the trail again, next big stop Wichita, Kansas.

On the way to Wichita we passed through a place where there were a bunch of mounds of dirt built up. It looked kinda scary and strange and I asked my great scout Cal about em.

"No idea," was his entire explanation.

I found out much later that they were made by a really ancient Indian tribe that no one really knew much about.

For reasons I have never figured out, I had always dreamed of riding a raft on a river. So when we came to a good sized river a couple of days east of Wichita, I found a man with the likely name of Clifford, who happened to own a raft for taking folks across. We settled on a price for the transport of two humans and two horses and pushed off from shore. The result, as I mentioned, was rather poor, and now we found ourselves wet, tired and still needing a way across the river.

My great scout Cal recommended that we ride along the southern shore of the river until we found a wide shallow section that we could ride across. I didn't appreciate it that he also said that it was what he wanted to do in the first place.

If I had any doubts about Cal's knowledge, which I did, they disappeared when we found a spot in the river that was exactly how Cal had described it. It was a lot wider than other parts of the river and was no more than knee deep on a horse at the deepest part. Half way across the river a belated thought struck me and I asked Cal, "If our horses were such great swimmers, why did we have to find a shallow spot? Why couldn't we just swim them across any ol' place?"

"So we could dry out a little," was all he said. Guess it made sense too. Sort of.

Soon as we got to the other shore I heard a bunch of sounds like I never heard before. There was a bunch of shouting and whistling combined with the bellows of what sounded like a million head of cattle. Every once in a while I heard a loud crack, like a gunshot but it turned out to be whips. I got so curious about the commotion that I stopped Wind and turned him in the direction of the noise so I could catch sight of the herd.

Cal stopped and looked too but he must have seen a herd before because he didn't look all that curious. Wind acted up in a way I'd never seen him do before. He acted like he wanted to run up in the herd. I had to hold him back he wanted to go so bad. When Cal noticed it he said, "Let him go. Let's see what kind a cow horse he is." He must have recognized the behavior in Wind.

So I let up on the reins and ol' Wind took off like his namesake. This was only the second time I'd ridden him flat out, and I had almost forgotten what the thrill was like. Now that I was reminded, I whooped and laughed like a little kid and laid out over his neck, hangin on, once again, for dear life.

Wind ran toward the herd like they were his long lost relatives. I couldn't wait to see what he would do once he caught up with them, and he was catching up fast. Turned out it was a little too fast. What with me and Wind goin hell bent for leather, and me whoopin and hollerin, and ol Cal comin up behind us with a look on his face more like desperation than determination, the cowboys tending the herd thought that they were being rustled or stampeded or both.

Cal, being experienced at cow tending, belatedly realized how the cowboys would interpret my rushing them, and he was tryin hard to catch up to us and warn us. But there ain't many horses can ever catch up to Wind when he's let loose, so all Cal managed to do was add to the conclusions of the cowpokes that they were being set upon.

My first awareness that there was any sort of a problem was when one of the cow punchers pulled a rifle from his saddle scabbard and took aim at me. I suppose he chose me over Cal since I was the closest. At that moment, if I thought I could have stopped Wind on a dime and spun him around, I would have done just that. But a horse on a tear don't do much of anything very suddenly.

The only thing I could think to do was bail out of the saddle. There was a chance the fall might kill me, but it was less of a chance than that of a bullet, so off I went. And just in time too, because I think I caught the wind of a bullet just past my head when I jumped. The timing of the bullet coming at the same moment I jumped probably made the shooter think he hit me, which was lucky for me but might be unlucky for Cal if he became his next target.

My worry for Cal's well being was rudely interrupted by a sudden encounter with the ground. The impact didn't turn out to be deadly but it did turn out to be painful. Fortunately I didn't break anything bigger than a butt cheek, and I had already gotten used to sore butt cheeks.

Next to Cal my first concern was for Wind. I hoped, first of all that he didn't get shot, and second of all that he would stop runnin sometime before he got to the Atlantic Ocean.

After hitting the dirt I didn't move. Not because I was smart that way, but because I was too stunned to move, which was another piece of damn good luck for me. It gave the cowboys a chance to reconsider, and hopefully become a little less bloody minded.

I didn't hear any more shooting while I was layin in the dust so I took it for a good sign that Cal hadn't been shot. Then I heard a horse steppin near my head and I looked up at some horse legs, happy to see that it was The General.

"You OK?" I heard Cal ask.

I looked further up and saw Cal.

"Mostly," I said.

"You're lucky," he said.

"How do you figure," I asked him. I myself could think of several aspects to my luck, but I wanted to hear his version.

"I used to work for this outfit and one of them recognized me just in time." That was a version I had never considered.

"Sounds like it's more lucky for you than for me," I pointed out.

"Good point. Lucky for both of us in the end I reckon," he said.

I was about to ask him if he seen Wind when I felt his nose nudge me in the back. I was still lyin in the dirt so I drug my bones upright and scratched him under the chin, which, I had discovered some time before, he liked.

"How far did he run before stoppin?" I asked Cal.

"Funny thing. He put on the brakes as soon as you left the saddle, never got more than ten feet past you. In fact he's been standing over you this whole time. Only just now nudged you to get your attention," Cal told him.

I was impressed by Wind's loyalty, but before I had a chance to express it the cowboys had caught up to us and started asking questions. Cal greeted the ones he knew and they, in turn, introduced him to the ones he didn't. Then everyone was introduced to me, which didn't impress them much.

What did impress them was Wind. And no one could blame them for that. These men put a powerful value on good horses and they always took notice of a good one when they saw one.

Their destination for that day was the river we had just crawled out of. We trailed along and camped with them that night on the eastern bank. The cattle were easy to manage, since they were thirsty and had plenty of river water to keep them occupied. So we spent the evening around the fire and exchanged stories. Mostly I was asked about Wind but there was little I could tell them that they couldn't see for themselves.

I found out that the herd had started at a ranch in Northwest Texas and was headed for Wichita to be shipped east on the train. Normally they would have followed the Chisholm trail which ran a little further west, but they'd heard there was trouble with rustlers so they took a different trail more to the east and ended up here.

We told them we were headed for Dodge City and asked if we could go along with them as far as Wichita. They said it was fine with them as long as we didn't mind workin for our grub along the way. We agreed and when darkness came we rolled out our sugguns for the night.

# CHAPTER FIFTEEN

*THE MORNING COMES MIGHTY EARLY* in a cow camp and we were astir before daylight. Camp cooky had plenty of hot coffee brewed already, and we could smell the bacon and the beans cookin alongside the beef and hotcakes. Cowboys can really eat at breakfast, and these boys shoveled it in by the pound. It's likely to be the only real meal in a long day so if you don't fill up at breakfast you'll end up mighty hungry later on. Cal and I were no exception as we filled up on our first pay check with the Rockin R Rafter outfit.

I commented on the quality of the grub to one of the hands and asked him if camp food was always so good. He said it depended on the cook and was only as good as camp cooky's aim to please, and then walked off towards his horse. I silently thanked God that we had a camp cooky aimin to please.

Once the cows were stood up and gathered a bit, the lead steer was pushed across the river by the boss, who was also the point man in this case. Being the Johnny Newcombs, me and Cal had to ride drag. It was an unpopular job because of all the dust you had to eat while doing it, but I eventually found out that it was important nonetheless.

Since I had no idea what to do on a cattle drive I started out by staying close to Cal, trying to do whatever it was that I saw him doing. That turned out not to be so easy. Not because of any difficult maneuvers he was doing, but because Wind seemed to be having his own ideas about what to do. He refused to obey my signals and went off in any direction which suited him. I was struggling to keep him under my control when Cal rode by me in a rush and, without slowing down, hollered at me to let Wind have his head.

Thinking Cal, or most anyone else, knew best about these things I followed his advice and gave Wind a free rein. And brother what a ride he gave me. I nearly fell off him three times in the first three minutes. He jumped out after the first cow he saw that began to stray from the main herd and I nearly came out the back end of the saddle from the suddenness of it. Then when he caught up to the animal he skidded to a halt right in front of it, which almost pitched me out of the saddle again. Then he dodged back and forth with such quick movements, trying to keep that cow from getting around him, that I was forced to hold the saddle horn with both hands to stay in my seat, which later earned me the name White Knuckle Willy from the boys of the Rockin R Rafter.

It went on like that all day long and, just like all the rest of the cowboys, I was too busy with the workings of my horse and the cattle to have time to palaver with any of the boys, including Cal. It was long, hard, tiring, dusty, thirsty work, and halfway through the day I was so weak I thought I might not make it to the next camp. In spite of that I was having so much fun whirling around on Winds superb back that the tiredness felt more like a good feeling than a bad one and I somehow managed to finish off the day.

Around the fire that evening there was a lot of admiration of Winds ability to work cattle. He became the dominant subject of conversation and nothing much was said about anything I had done that day. I didn't resent it though because I was just as bedazzled by Wind as everyone else, and I had the extra advantage of bein his owner which made me real proud.

## CHAPTER SIXTEEN

*THE NEXT MORNING, WHEN COOKY BANGED* on a tin plate to wake us up, I found it hard to move around. Every part of me was stiff and sore, and some parts were extra sore. The only thing that didn't hurt was my butt, which struck me as funny. Lots of jokes were made at my expense when the other hands noticed the way I was moving. I let them get away with funnin me because, well, mainly because any one of them could lick me, and also because I knew they had all had their turn at being made fun of when they did their fist day on a drive.

Cal and I rode drag again and by the end of the second day I was starting to get the hang of how riding drag worked. By the third morning I was just as sore as the second, but a few days later I was in shape and didn't feel sore.

It was on that first sore-less day that we arrived in Wichita. We put the herd in the pens at the rail yard and some of us went into town for food and a drink, while a couple of top hands stayed with the herd. The herd boss, Antonio Flores, stayed behind to do the dealins with the stock yard and railroad. He would meet us in town later.

The town wasn't like I'd pictured it. It wasn't as big and most of the buildings that existed were shoddy-built wood plank affairs. Some of the buildings were no more than glorified tents. The people weren't how I pictured neither. There were lots of cowboys around, which was how I did picture it, but there were also a bunch of other type folks. The other types seemed to belong to one of two categories. They were either shop owners and such, or they were hanging around town without much purpose that I could make out, except maybe to make trouble. A couple of the hang-arounds I saw gave me an uneasy feeling and I thought they might be the kind of bad men pa had warned me about. I made the easy decision to do all I could to avoid them.

There was also a possible third category, prostitutes, but there were not many of them and they looked wore out and had sad looks in their eyes that made me feel sorry for them. I didn't fear them like the ones I'd seen in Terry Oats, but I still wouldn't get too near them either.

Cal was with me when we walked the town and he commented on the women. "Them gals remind me of a dog who gets nothin but beatings from its owner," he said.

It was a fair description. "Let's get a drink," I suggested.

"Ok," Cal said, but he had an uncertain look on his face and I regretted my suggestion. I had forgotten that it wasn't too long ago he had a problem with likker.

"Maybe we should eat first," I said. "Drivin cattle makes me hungry."

"Ok," he said again, but this time he looked more happy about it.

We drug our butts around town looking for some place halfway decent to eat. We didn't have much luck and when we asked a local merchant for advice he told us that the town was in a sort of depression at present. Apparently, according to this merchant, things haven't been the same since the railroad landed in Doge City, and "that Wyatt Earp fella" left town a few years back.

Of course we heard of Wyatt Earp. The whole dang world heard of him. "Did you know him," I asked.

"Yes I did, young man, but I don't brag on it. I'm more proud of the fact that he left our town. Man only caused trouble for us as far as I'm concerned," the merchant said. I didn't remind him of the fact that he had just told me the depression occurred after Earp's departure.

# CHAPTER SEVENTEEN

*THE MERCHANT HAD POINTED US TO A PLACE* to eat called the Longhorn Eatery and Saloon. We went there, and the sight of it didn't improve my appetite. It smelled more like a saloon, or something worse, than an Eatery and it was loud. I mean so loud I had to shout at Cal if I wanted him to hear what I was saying. It was full of drunk cowboys who were somehow unable to speak in low volume, and the piano was going, and the card players had to shout every time they won a hand. And every time they lost one too.

Not knowing anywhere else to find grub we stayed at the Longhorn and set at a table, waiting for a barmaid. None showed up, but the bartender yelled at us across the room, asking what we wanted. I don't know how he was able to be heard across that distance, but I doubted my ability to shout loud enough for him to hear my answer. Lucky for me Cal had some experience at this and hollered back, with amazing volume, that we was hungry.

The bartender nodded, indicating he had gotten our order. Then, while we were waiting for the meal, a pretty Mexican gal brought out a whiskey bottle and two glasses and set them on our table. We didn't order drinks and I was not prepared for being served them without asking. Especially I was not prepared for how to deal with Cal on the matter. But worse than that, I was not ready for how I reacted to the Mexican girl.

When I first saw her my heart sped up and I found myself staring at her. She noticed my stare and gave me a little smile, and that undid me. I probably turned a pretty deep shade of red and I had to look away so as to keep my composure.

Cal laughed at me, then grabbed the bottle and a glass and poured a drink. Then he tipped the bottle toward my glass and raised his eyebrows at me, inquiring if I wanted one. Not bein prepared for any of this I dealt with it in my usual manner – I avoided it.

"Sure, pour me a shot," I said.

I sipped my whiskey and considered my situation. I had gotten kind of fond of Cal over the past few months. I guess in a way I saved his bacon back in St. Louis, and he had sure saved my bacon a couple of times on the trail. And I hated to think he might be slippin back into his old habits, but I wasn't sure how to stop him.

I wrestled with the problem for a while and finally came up with a solution. It was probably a good solution, but I didn't like it. So I wrestled with the problem some more. And I came up with the same solution, but I didn't like it any better. Like it or not, I knew it was the right thing to do. I had to face him head on with the matter and tell him to leave the likker alone. Problem was that I was afraid to do it. Not scared really, but just not comfortable with buttin in to his business. The fact that I had done just that in St. Louis didn't help much neither. It just made me more confused. As it turned out I didn't need to worry about it after all, for two reasons.

The sudden quiet that came over the previously noisy saloon was as loud as a gunshot due to the extreme change. I turned my head in the same direction everyone else had and saw the reason for the hush. Our herd boss Antonio had just entered the place.

I wasn't sure why his appearance would silence the place like it did. There sure wasn't any let up of the noise when Cal and I came into the place.

Antonio spotted us and walked toward our table, cool eyes of the others in the room following him the whole way. There was something about him that they didn't like, no doubt about that. There was no mistakin the hate in the room.

"Have a seat boss," I said as he approached us.

"Thanks," he said and sat in the extra chair. I was sure he was aware of the reactions in the room but if he was bothered by it he didn't show it.

There were only two glasses at our table, mine and Cal's. Cal slid his over in front of the boss and that's when I noticed that Cal hadn't touched it. I made a mental note to tell him later that I was proud of his temperance.

"Thanks," Antonio said.

I know I had learned a good lesson about not buttin into a man's affairs and all, but I was pretty sure the current situation was a bona fide exception to the rule.

"Seems to me you have some sort of reputation around here," I said to him.

"Something like that," Antonio said. Then he drank his shot of whiskey in one swallow. Cal poured him another one.

76

"I'm not trying to butt in where I shouldn't," I said, "But you're sittin at our table and it sure feels a whole lot like trouble in here right now. So I figure I might have a right to ask."

"You're right, Patrick," he answered. "You got the right, and I'll tell you the story." Here he paused to take another shot of whiskey, and by the time he finished it there was a man standing by our table who didn't look like he wanted to give Antonio a chance to tell his tale. In fact he looked like he wanted to make sure Antonio never said another word again.

That was when I was sure I was looking at the kind of man pa had warned me about, and I realized he was right. By instinct I knew for sure the man was pure evil, even while my mind tried to tell me not to accept the truth of it. What pa never said, but I learned right then, was that my mind didn't want to accept it because it was so damn terrifying. I wished the man was something other than what I knew he was, because what he was was hell on horseback, and it was only pa's warning that kept me alive that day.

I stood up out of my chair so fast that it fell over. Hell on horseback must have thought I was making a play for him and he cleared leather with his gun, his evil eyes burning his hatred for me. He wasn't foolin, he would kill me, so I tipped up the table and threw it toward him, hoping to at least throw his aim off a bit.

I didn't wear a holstered gun back then, but Cal did, and when the evil stranger reached for his gun Cal stood and reached for his. By accident, when I threw the table up it hit Cal's gun while he was drawing it, throwing his aim off and his bullet went wild. At the same instant the table also hit the bad man's gun, deflecting his aim and the bullet smashed into Cal's chest, killing him almost instantly.

Antonio was also heeled and had drawn quickly, shooting the bad guy almost at the same time Cal got hit.

Smoke filled the room, which was dead quiet now, and it stung my eyes. I stared at Cal's dead body on the floor, blinkin back smoky tears, not knowin what to do, and not wanting to believe he was dead. I expected him to get up any second, but when he didn't I looked at Antonio for an explanation.

The boss didn't offer an explanation. He held his gun in one hand, leveled at the room in case the murderer had any friends in the room. No one else made a move so he grabbed me by the arm and drug me out the door. The last thing I saw on our way out was the pretty girl who brought out our whiskey starin at me with a worried look.

I found out later that the man who killed Cal was named Murphy, and he did indeed have some friends in the saloon. I heard them shouting and running towards us as we caught up our horses and swung up in the saddles. A couple of the Rockin R Rafter boys, who were standing guard on the herd, had heard the shots and seen us running hell bent for leather toward them, had jumped up on their horses and were ready to ride.

# CHAPTER EIGHTEEN

*ANTONIO KNEW HOW IT WORKED* in these kinds of towns, and these situations, and he knew word would get around fast to the rest of the outfit about what had happened. Early in their history together as an outfit he had explained to the crew certain plans in case of certain emergencies, this being the one.

As the four of us rode hard out of town, the rest of the gang was getting the news and carryin out the previously agreed upon instructions. Half of them armed themselves with guns and lots of ammunition and stood watch over the herd, in case anyone got the idea it was up for grabs now. They were the best men with guns and so the duty fell to them.

The rest of the gang rode out of town in different directions, but all intending to end up at the same agreed upon meeting place, which was a hollow in the bluff overlooking the Arkansas river about a mile downstream from town.

It only took thirty minutes for the group to unite in the hollow. The whole crew was there. The ones watching the herd were outnumbered by Murphy's friends and were forced to abandon the herd, risking losing it if they couldn't return for it. A sentry was immediately assigned atop the bluff to watch the back trail and send a warning of approaching riders.

I was in shock for the whole ride and, in spite of the fact that I had ridden my own horse to the meeting place, I couldn't recall it. Everything that had happened in the last thirty minutes had to be related to me after we had arrived and dismounted.

My only thoughts were of Cal, and Antonio had to resort to dousing me with a cup of water in my face to get my attention. It worked and I listened to what he had to say.

"I'm really sorry about Cal," he said. "We all liked him. But we have to think about ourselves right now if we don't want to join him just yet. I need you to concentrate so that we can do what we need to do to survive this. Can you do that for me?"

"Yes," I said. "But you'll have to tell me what to do." I was in no condition to think for myself.

"Good, because I'm going to ask you to do something very brave. It will be dangerous. You think you are up to it?"

"Yes," I answered quickly. Later, when I thought back on this day, I realized I did not say yes because I really wanted to be brave. I said it because I was still in shock and words were just coming out of my mouth without me thinking.

"Ok, here's what I want you to do. You have the only horse that can do this. I want you to ride out in the trail and when those guys show up I want them to chase you. They will think you are the greenhorn, which you are, and so they will think you are riding in the rear, and they will chase you thinking that the rest of us will be a short way ahead of you. They can never catch you on Wind. No horse can ever catch Wind, so you'll outrun them. But they will be shooting at you so stay low on his neck and don't give them a target."

"Ok, I can do that, but then what?"

"As soon as their horses tire they will pull them up and turn back. But you keep going, don't stop. They will only be resting their horses, and then they will keep tracking you down. Just ride as far as you can without killing your horse, then make camp somewhere out of sight. And don't make a fire or any kind of noise until we find you."

"How you going to find me after all that?" I wondered.

Antonio smiled. His smile said 'You obviously don't know me'.

"Don't worry," he said, "I can find you blindfolded. But before we catch up to you we will take care of the fellas who are chasin you."

"Ok, I'll do it. When do I leave?"

"Give your horse some rest for now. Our lookout will give us a heads up when they come in sight. Then you ride. You rest now too. You'll need it."

# PART THREE: THE RIDE

A human being is constantly changing,
And yet he is always and only
Exactly who he is.

Doc Bonner

## CHAPTER NINETEEN

*THAT DAY I RODE. MAN DID I RIDE.* When the lookout gave the signal I headed down a trail that was more than a horse race against death. It was that as well, for sure, because I had to dodge plenty of bullets. Each time I heard a gunshot I thought it would be that last thing I ever heard and I tensed up for the impact of the bullet. I did that time after time, and a few times the bullets came close enough for me to hear them splitting the air as they passed by me.

Bullets weren't the only thing splitting the air, Wind was going faster than he ever had before. He seemed to sense the danger and the need to run. The ol' boy put more heart into running than I knew he had, and that's saying something. His legs were flyin so fast that his feet barely had time to stay on the ground and I felt like we were floating.

I was barely able to turn my head around to see where my pursuers might be, but I did manage it a time or two. The second time I looked they were losing ground, and the third time I looked they had stopped and were looking at me angrily and shaking their guns in the air. I had won that part of the race, now all I had to do was get far enough ahead of them to buy myself and the Rockin R Rafter outfit the time we needed to get clean away from those who wanted our hides.

I pulled Wind up into a normal gallop and kept the pace for as long as I could. I could tell Wind was wearin down some by the roughness of his gait. He was starting to struggle. And I was not in much better shape. My legs were shaky and I could feel a sharp pain in my knees each time I posted up in the saddle.

When I figured we were maybe three or four miles ahead of the where my pursuers had stopped I slowed Wind to a walk and started looking for a likely camp spot, like Antonio  asked me to. I saw a deer run up a hill to my left and then suddenly disappear. There must have been a depression or small canyon at that spot.

I followed the path of the deer and just as I suspected the land fell away into a shallow canyon. There were trees and water in the bottom and I decided to make camp there. I unsaddled Wind and let him drink and browse. I ate some jerky and drank a bit of the water.

The canyon wouldn't conceal me forever and I hoped that Antonio and his men would take care of the gang and find me before the bad guys did. All I could do now was wait, so I laid out a blanket. But before I rested I checked my gun to be sure it was loaded and I pulled a box of bullets out to have them handy. Then I put the gun in my holster and strapped it to my waist. I wasn't going to get caught unarmed again.

# CHAPTER TWENTY

*ANTONIO WAITED ABOUT FIVE MINUTES* after Patrick left and then lead his men out on the trail behind the avengers. His plan was simple and he hoped it would be effective. He wanted to come up behind the group of men who were chasing Patrick and shoot em down. Simple as that.

It would have worked too if Murphy's boss, Jens, had not been shrewd. Jens was one of the smartest men in the country, and possibly the most foul soul on earth. He thrived on death and mayhem. There were men who had decent reputations as killers who, after partnering with Jens for a while, would part company with him because he was too extreme for them. Antonio Flores was one of them. But what made Jens even more terrible as a human was that he was as shrewd as he was violent.

Jens had once worked with Antonio and he anticipated his maneuver. He kept half his men back and sent the other half to chase Patrick. When Antonio and his men came out of the hole they'd hid in, and onto the trail, Jens had them boxed in. He rode up behind them and started shooting.

Antonio's men started running down the trail toward Patrick but they didn't get far before runnin into the other half of Jens gang. The result was bloody and Antonio was shot several times by a laughing Jens. The rest of Antonio's men scattered and tried to run but they were all shot. Some kept riding for a ways but died later. Only one man, named Rowdy, made it clean away, and even he was wounded, shot in the thigh.

After the attack was over the spot became the scene of a bizarre celebration. The men hooted and hollered and shot their guns into the air. Some brought out whiskey bottles and others shot into the dead bodies nearby. A few men were robbing the dead on the ground. Jens smiled at the enjoyment some of his men were having. He knew some of them didn't enjoy what they were doing and only did it because Jens would kill them if they didn't, and that fact pleased him as well.

Jens let the boys have their fun until the whiskey was gone and the dead were stripped of all their valuables and then he rounded them up for their next job.

"Ok boys," he hollered, "Let's move out and go get us a horse." He was referring, of course, to Wind.

# CHAPTER TWENTY ONE

*AFTER PUTTING ON MY GUN* I laid back on my bed roll and waited. I knew I would never sleep because I was so nervous, so I stared up at the sky. It was the first time I had really paid attention to the stars and I was impressed by how dang many of them there were. At one point I thought I heard some shootin way far off and I hoped it was Antonio takin care of the gang. Then I started thinking about the Mexican gal.

About an hour after I heard the shooting, I thought I heard the sound of hooves on the ground at the top of the ridge. Wind looked nervously in the same direction so I got up and put my hand on my gun.

"Don't move," someone said from behind me. "And move your hand away from that gun. Real slow." I was surprised at the idea someone had gotten behind me without me hearing them, but I did what he said and lifted my hand slowly away from the holster. About that time a group of riders came over the ridge and down the hill into the little canyon, led by a big blond man.

The blond guy was tall but he wasn't lanky. His muscles bulged out every which way and there was no way of describing him other than ox strong. His hair was short cropped and there was a bald spot on his scalp that was a scar from some old wound. He smiled all the time but you could tell it wasn't because he was happy about something, unless it was the thought of killin someone. Murphy had scared me but this guy made me quiver with terror.

"You must be the greenhorn with the black horse I been hearin about," he said to me.

"What's your name boy?" he asked, still smiling the smile of death.

I didn't know if I would be able to speak until I heard the words coming out. "I'm Patrick McGee," I said faintly.

"Nice to meet you Patrick, I'm Jens, the man who is about to send you to meet your maker," he said. Then he drew his gun and aimed it at me. I jumped aside at the same instant he pulled the trigger and I felt an impact on my chest that was hard enough to spin me around and throw me off balance. As I was falling I heard another shot and a blow caught me on the back of the head, sending me into a void where awareness no longer exists.

# CHAPTER TWENTY TWO

*JOSEFINA WAS ALARMED WHEN JENS* and his men arrived back in Wichita, ready to have another celebration. They celebrated often, and each time was just as alarming as the previous ones. This time they were leading a prize horse and showing it off every chance they got. It took three ropes on it to keep it almost under control and when they tied it up in front of the saloon it ripped down the hitching post causing a mad scramble it the street. They finally cornered it in a box stall in the livery and came inside to brag about it. They usually got away with bragging openly about their illegal coups because they went largely unopposed in the town. There were too many of them and they were cold mean.

Josefina was tired of the high handed behavior of Jens and his men, and she was tired of the cowardly men in town who wouldn't oppose them. She constantly tried to figure out a way to get away from Wichita but had failed to come up with a plan so far.

Her boss at the saloon was an idiot but he wasn't as cruel as most, and he provided at least some form of protection. So she fought off the cowboys when she could and did what she had to when she couldn't. A woman alone was not such a good situation in Wichita at the current time. Lack of money wasn't keeping her here though, she'd saved up some. But she was too scared to leave on her own. She knew her boss would follow her if she left and then bring her back and punish her. Maybe worse. So she stayed. And prayed.

Then she had seen the handsome young man who came in to the saloon and had contributed to the killing of Murphy. She liked the way he smiled at her when she brought out their whiskey. She hated Murphy, who had a habit of abusing her, and was overjoyed when he got shot. And there was something about that man who threw the table at him, and had smiled at her. She couldn't get her mind off him.

After a while Jens group got so drunk, and therefore invincible, that they started bragging about the slaughter of the Rockin R Rafter cowboys, and the shooting of Patrick McGee, the previous owner of the black wonder horse. Josefina hadn't known the name of the man who smiled at her, but she knew he owned the black horse, and so she assumed he was the one they murdered. She was very saddened by the news.

A little later she heard her boss telling one of the Jens gang that he wouldn't want to be around when Shawn McGee found out about his son. Josefina asked what he meant by that and he explained to her that he once knew Shawn McGee, back in Richmond, and he wouldn't take his son's killing lightly.

News spread around town that Jens had successfully taken forced possession of yet another herd, and this time he had a bill of sale. That fact was somewhat surprising to anyone familiar with Jens' method. But what they didn't know was that he had kept an old bill of sale signed by Antonio when they had done a cattle deal earlier in their relationship. Jens, of course, had doctored the date on the document.

While his men were celebrating, Jens sold off the Rockin R Rafter herd, using his forged bill of sale. He deposited half the money in the bank under his own name and then split the rest with his crew, telling them it was the total proceeds of course.

Later that night, when Josefina got off work, she went to the telegraph office and sent a telegram to Shawn McGee. It was the least she could do for him.

# CHAPTER TWENTY THREE

*BACK IN RICHMOND, RILEY AND SHAWN* were drinking in Shawn's tavern when a messenger came in telling him he had an urgent cable from Wichita. They went together over to the telegraph office and received the message.

Riley watched as Shawn read the telegram and saw him turn white. Shawn dropped the telegram on the office floor and his eyes rolled back in his head. Riley grabbed him just in time to keep him from landing full force on the floor, out cold. While he waited for Shawn to come around he picked the telegram up off the floor and read it.

It was indeed devastating news and Riley couldn't blame Shawn for swooning. Here's how it read:

> To Shawn McGee stop report that Patrick McGee murdered by
> Jens Olsen stop part of a cattle rustling operation stop all members
> of Rockin R Rafter outfit believed killed stop signed Josefina.

The telegram left a lot of questions, but the one important fact that was not in doubt was the murder of Shawn's son, Patrick.

# CHAPTER TWENTY FOUR

*WHEN I WOKE UP I ALMOST WISHED I HADN'T.* The small bit of light I could see burned into my eyes and caused my head to hurt so bad that I felt sick. I closed my eyes but my head didn't feel a whole lot better. I was on the edge of sleep and awake, and could have easily escaped back into the painless world of unconsciousness. But first I had to see if Wind was okay.

I opened my eyes again, moaning from the pain of it, and lifted my head to look for Wind, but that little effort took it all out of me and I blacked out again. I don't know how long I was out. Could have been a minute or could have been a week, but it only seemed like a second and When I woke, I again looked for Wind.

"They took him," I heard someone say. It was a weak voice, like it might sound if I tried to speak. But it weren't me.

Curious, I carefully turned my head in the direction of the voice. It hurt, like before, but I didn't black out this time. I noticed a campfire going, and I was sure I hadn't started it. The brightness of the fire hurt my head and I squinted against the glow. The voice had come from the other side of the flames, and what with my partial blindness and weak condition I couldn't see around them to make out who it was that spoke. And I sure didn't stand a chance of standing up and walking around the fire.

"If you're lookin for your horse," the voice said again, "they took him. Jens and his gang took off with him after they shot you up."

I reckon I blacked out again because the next thing I remembered it was daylight. There was still a fire going though, and I seen a man sitting on the ground bending over it stirring a pot. Something about that was odd. I'd never seen a man tend a fire while sitting on the ground. Usually a body would squat over a fire, or set on a stump or something.

"Now that smells damn good," I said after getting a whiff of the coffee that was boiling in the pot. Then I saw the blood caked up on the pants of the man making the coffee and reckoned it was why he wasn't squatting.

"Well, you must feel a sight better if you can see, smell, speak and drink coffee," the man said.

"Reckon you're right," I said. " 'Cept I still feel like a pile of warmed over horseshit."

"I don't doubt it," he said. "You're lucky you're alive enough to feel like a pile of any kind of shit." He started pouring a cup of coffee and I wondered which one of us might be able to get up long enough to get it in my hand.

"Can you move?" I asked him.

"It ain't easy, and it hurts like hell, but I can if I have to," he said. Then he sort of half shuffled and half dragged himself close enough to me to hand me the cup. I was almighty thankful to get a steaming hot cup of coffee.

"Thanks, mister. I can really use this. Sorry I couldn't come retrieve it on my own but I ain't even sure how long I'll stay awake much less how I could move around."

"Name's Rowdy, and bad off as I am you're worse off, so don't worry about it. Jens boys shot me up too. Hell, we'll both be lucky to live long enough to enjoy a few more cups of coffee." I recognized him then, after he said his name. He was one of Antonio's outfit.

I sipped some coffee and then carefully ran a finger along the back of my head. There was a lot of blood caked on the back of my head and neck and it was tender. There was a deep gash on my scalp but no hole in my skull. So I guessed most of my brains were still where they belonged, but maybe a bit rattled around.

"Bullet bounced off your skull," Rowdy said. "That's why you ain't singin with the angels right now. But it knocked you out good, and that's why you been blacked out so much. You'll live through that though. It's the hole in your chest you best be worried about, you may not make it through that bullet."

My head injury had me so worried that I hadn't paid much attention to what had been done to my chest by the first bullet. I looked at my shirt, which was soaked in blood, and seen that someone, probably Rowdy, had pulled it back from the wound and put a bandage on the bullet hole.

"I did the best I could but I don't know much about doctorin," Rowdy said. "Besides, I ain't in much condition myself to do a lot. Jens' men got me in the leg and I lost a lot of blood. Might have an infection too."

"Thanks for whatever you done. Must have been hard on you. I don't reckon the bullet in my chest hit anything too vital though, otherwise I wouldn't be alive," I said.

"Maybe not, but you ain't out of the woods yet. Could be bleedin inside and if the bleedin don't get ya the fever might. I seen a it happen a couple of times," Rowdy informed me.

"Ain't we a pair," I said. "You bring anything besides coffee?"

"Nope, I didn't have time to gather supplies when I was runnin for my life."

"I reckon so," I said.

# CHAPTER TWENTY FIVE

*JOSEFINA LEFT THE TELEGRAPH OFFICE* after sending a message to Shawn, but she still could not get her mind off Patrick. And now that she knew his name it was even harder for her to avoid his memory. She felt she should do more for him and his father than just send a telegram. Jens men had probably left Patrick's body layin beside the trail, and she thought maybe she should get it and have it sent home.

She took off her apron and started out the door of the saloon. Her boss, Andrew, asked where the hell she was going, since it was still working hours for her. She told him she was going to pick up the laundry from the chinaman. Andrew said OK and told her to hurry back.

Josefina chuckled to herself. There was no Chinese laundry person in Wichita, and she made a game of telling such lies to her boss routinely, just to prove how stupid he was.

Instead of picking up laundry she saddled her own horse and led a borrowed one down the trail to find Patrick's body. She would use the borrowed horse to pack his body back, but used it now to haul some sheets and blankets for wrapping the body, and a bit of food for her to eat on the trail. It was a chore she did not relish, and she could not imagine how to deal with the sight of his corpse, but she felt compelled to do something for a man who had stirred feelings in her for the first time in a long time.

She rode for several hours without seeing a body and started to wonder if she had missed something along the trail. It was possible that it was further along though, so she kept on. Some time later, when she was sure she'd ridden farther than the killing could possibly have taken place, she turned back, thinking that she either failed to see something or that the gang had moved the body somewhere else. It was only a moment after she turned back that she smelled smoke.

# CHAPTER TWENTY SIX

*IN RICHMOND, RILEY WAS HELPING SHAWN* ready two of Shawn's strongest horses for what would be a hard journey west. So hard that he needed two top horses, which required less resting time. Even then he would only be riding to Terre Haute, where he would board a train for the rest of the distance to Wichita.

When Shawn had first told Riley that he was going to Wichita it frightened him a little. He wondered if Shawn intended to confront the gang that shot his son, and if he did, Riley thought there was a good chance he would not come out on top of such a confrontation.

Riley had asked him what he intended to do once he got to Wichita and Shawn had refused to reply, thus multiplying Riley's worries.

Of course news of Patrick's murder spread quickly in Richmond and had the predictable effect of elevating his reputation from hero to martyr. Various townspeople were conducting various events and ceremonies intended to intern his memory into the immortal annals of history. The mayor proclaimed the date of his death as a recognized holiday in perpetuity.

"I wish you'd reconsider," Riley said as Shawn stepped into the saddle. "There ain't nothing you can do for him no more. Just let them ship the body back here and let's bury him proper."

His plea had little effect and Shawn didn't even acknowledge he'd heard it. He just spurred his horse and rode, ponying his extra mount behind. Riley shook his head and swore under his breath.

## CHAPTER TWENTY SEVEN

*I FINISHED MY CUP OF COFFEE* and then blacked out again. In my fever dreams I danced with the pretty Mexican girl from the saloon in Wichita. When I woke up the pain was the first thing to announce itself to me. I moaned and avoided opening my eyes.

"You still there, Rowdy?" I asked.

"Yeah, I'm here," he answered.

"What's that smell?" I asked, after smelling something other than coffee on the fire.

"It's food," he said.

"Smells like heaven," I said. "I thought you said you didn't have any food."

"That's what I said sure enough," he said.

That was good enough reason for me to risk opening my eyes, but when I tried, all I saw was black. I panicked.

"I'm blind Rowdy! I can't see!" I tried to sit up, reaching out with my hands to see if I could feel something, but the pain in my chest put me down again.

"Ju yust no move, senor Patrick," I heard a female voice say. "Ju will make bandage no good if ju move. Ju are no blind. I put bandage on ju head."

I froze. Not because she ordered me to, but because she was a she.

I opened my mouth and then shut it again several times, unable to come up with a response that I might consider to be not embarrassing. So instead of sounding idiotic I managed to look like a fish out of water, not much more impressive than sounding dumb I imagine, but it's what I did so there you go.

I didn't move and I didn't speak for a minute or so, then a touch of a hand on my forehead startled me.

"It's OK," the female voice said, "I yust check for feber. Ju are bery hot, senor. I take bandage off ju cabeza so ju can eat."

I felt the bandage unwinding off my head and when I could focus again the first thing I saw was the pretty Mexican girl from the saloon. I

96

wasn't too sure about what fever she had been talking about when she felt my forehead, but I sure as hell felt my face start to burn when I looked into the eyes of the gal of my dream.

"Thanks, ma'am," I stuttered.

She handed me a bowl of hot broth and said, "Ju eat this, then I give ju more food what is not water, si?"

I spooned broth into my mouth while staring at the girl all the while. She was true to her word and after I finished off the broth she brought me some beans and bread. Between servings I had noticed that my chest wound had been cleaned and bandaged. When I glanced at Rowdy I seen his leg was bandaged too, and he had a bit of color coming back to his skin.

"Did you doctor us up?" I asked her.

"Si," she said.

"Thank you," I mumbled humbly.

"Ju yust eat," she said. But I thought I might have detected a smile forming on her incredible lips. The thought of those lips was the last thing I was aware of before I went back out again.

What followed was three days of deep fever, when dreams and awake times are not able to be known one from the other. I shivered uncontrollably for hours and then burned up and sweated for more hours before shivering again. The dreams were never good, and sometimes were what bein in hell might have been like.

On the fourth day I was awake and I knew it, but I was almighty weak and I ached everywhere. The Mexican gal was still there and she was spooning broth into my mouth.

I managed to whisper, "What's your name?"

"Josefina," she said.

## CHAPTER TWENYT EIGHT

*SHAWN'S JOURNEY WEST SHOULD REALLY* be called something other than just a ride. It was even more than a quest. It would more correctly be called a madness. He was riding wild with his sorrow, burning deep in his fiber. When he rode through a town people got hurriedly out of his way at just the sight of him. Women grabbed their children by the arm and drug them into the closest building, then shut and locked the door.

There was a foreboding that preceded his physical presence, and his physical presence, when it arrived, overpowered the foreboding that preceded it. The hard, blank, steely glint in his eyes, and the angry pain in his face warned anyone who he came near to steer clear and not to cross him.

In Terre Haute, when he tried to buy a train ticket, and the agent had told him that the train was sold out, all it took was one hard look from Shawn and the agent instantly cleared a car for him. He was shaking and sweating by the time he handed Shawn a ticket, and Shawn had never uttered a word to the man.

When he got off the train in Wichita he rode through town asking anyone he saw where he might find Jens Olsen. Only one person was brave enough to answer him, or stupid enough, take your pick, the rest turned and ran. That person told Shawn to check with Andrew at the Cattleman's Saloon.

Andrew was behind the bar when he saw Shawn enter. At the first glimpse of him Andrew knew trouble was at his doorstep. He reached quickly under the bar and brought up his ten gauge. His fear intensified when Shawn seemed not to even notice the cannon he was holding and instead walked boldly straight into the path of it.

"Where's Jens?" Shawn demanded.

"Howdy, Mr. McGee," Andrew stuttered. "You recall meeting me once in Richmond some time back?"

Shawn ignored his question and said, "I'm only going to ask you one more time. Where's Jens?"

There was no doubt in Andrews mind what the consequences for not answering would be, and even the shotgun gave him no sense of security.

"I don't know exactly where they are at this moment but I know that they are somewhere along the Chisholm trail, south of Dodge City. That's all I know and it's the truth," Andrew answered wisely.

Shawn spun on his boot heels and walked out, never acknowledging Andrew. Andrew considered, very briefly, shooting him in the back with the ten gauge, but the mans demeanor had so unnerved him that he feared his dead spirit would come back and kill him somehow.

A few hours later, as Shawn rode away from Wichita toward Dodge, he smelled smoke. Since he could not see a fire from the trail he suspected that whoever lit the fire was not wanting to be seen. That possibility led to the possibility that it could be Jens, who, in his mind was a wanted outlaw, hiding from the law. He obviously hadn't been in Wichita long enough to become familiar with Jens' hold on the town and his flaunting disregard for the law.

Shawn dismounted and followed the smoke trail on foot, working his way up the low ridge as quietly as possible. When he topped the ridge and stuck his eyes up over it to get a look, he was starin at the business end of a Colt 44. He was stunned, not so much by the gun as he was by the young girl who was holding it.

"Ju yust no move, senor," she said.

"How'd you know I was comin?" Shawn asked, amazed that he could have been heard or seen.

"Me caballo, senor," she said. "My horse he hear something. I trust my horse, senor."

"Smart woman," Shawn said.

Josefina led Shawn down the hill into camp, at gun point. Rowdy and Patrick had been watching Josefina breathlessly, hoping Jens hadn't come back to finish the job of killing them. When Patrick realized who it was she was bringing into camp he felt tears coming to his eyes and he tried to rise up, but his body failed him and he fell back.

"Pa?" he managed to moan.

"Patrick? Is that really you? Oh my god." Shawn rushed to Patrick's side.

# CHAPTER TWENTY NINE

*SEEING MY PA WALK DOWN THAT HILL* did something to my spirit that I will never be able to understand or explain. My whole outlook on life changed the second I saw him, and I had regained more hope than I realized I had lost.

After the shock of the surprise had worn off for us both we settled down by the fire. Pa sat while I laid with my head resting in his lap. Having him tend to me like that was both strange and familiar at the same time. I felt the familiarity that only a father/son can feel with each other, but it had been so long since we had that kind of personal contact that it was also a little strange. All in all I enjoyed the sensation it gave me.

Not much else happened for the next two days, at least not that I can recall very well. I slept most of the time, and when I wasn't sleeping I ate meals or drank coffee or water. I heard a little talk between Pa and Rowdy whenever Josefina woke me to change my bandages or tend my wounds, but I didn't converse with the others except to say how I was doing or how I was feeling, and things of that nature.

On the third day after Pa got there I was able to sit up a while and tend to a few of my own basic needs, but when I tried to stand up and walk I didn't get too far. Slowly and with lots of pain I managed to stand, and once there I was determined not to waste the effort without walking so I took a couple of steps. The return trip to the ground took a lot less time and I was sweating and shaking from the effort.

After that I slept some more and when I awoke we all sat around the fire and talked, each of us wanting their own set of questions answered. I had a few of my own for Pa and Rowdy, but the greatest amount of my curiosity revolved around Josefina. I could hardly think of anything else.

First I told Pa about how I got caught up in the killing of Cal and Murphy back in town, and then how Jens chased me down and shot me, and then took Wind.

Once Pa learned Josefina's name he figured out she was the one who sent the telegram to Richmond. Josefina confirmed this and told her version of what happened in the saloon when Cal got shot. She also told us everything she heard Jens and his gang say when they returned to town with Wind.

Even though my mind was obsessed with wanting to know all about Josefina, my tongue was never coordinated enough to get any words out. It was much easier to ask Rowdy some of the questions I had been wondering about for days.

"How'd you get shot up Rowdy?" I asked.

"Jens men done it," he answered. "I was with Antonio when they ambushed us. I think I am the only one who made it out alive, and I damn near didn't."

"How did you find me?" I asked.

"Antonio told us all where you were likely to be holed up before we left, just in case he got shot or something." He looked sad when said it.

"I'm sorry about the boss," I said. "He was good to me and Cal. You must have liked him."

"Yes," he said sadly. I could tell he was struggling with some emotion about it.

"What's the story behind the hatred of him that I noticed in Wichita?" I asked.

"It ain't Wichita that hated him so much as it is Jens. And right now Wichita is Jens town. There's a history between Jens and Antonio. I don't know as I ever heard all the details but what I did hear was that they used to be partners. And from what I hear they was rustlin cattle.

"My way of figurin was that the boss started off like most rustlers do, he needed to earn a little money and thought rustlin would be an easy way to get it. He thought it would be a one time only thing, just to get him on his feet, then he could go on the straight and narrow. A poor strategy to start with but then he was unlucky enough to hook up with Jens, and by the time he found out what the man was like he had gotten involved in way more crime and violence than he imagined.

"He finally quit the gang after Jens shot down a couple of cowboys without cause. The two cowboys was camped along the trail, and posed no threat to Jens or anyone, but he just rode up to their camp and shot em without warning. It was just cold blooded meanness, evil for the sake of evil so to speak."

I glanced at pa at this point and he gave me a meaningful nod, like he was sayin 'see, I told you so'.

Rowdy continued, "Shortly after Antonio left the gang a posse caught up with Jens in one of his hideouts. They escaped the posse but Jens thought it was Antonio who told them where he was hiding. Antonio never did tell anyone about the hideout but Jens never believed otherwise and had it in for him from then on out."

"Well, that explains a lot," I said. I thought about how Jens had killed them two cowboys, and how similar it was to what he tried with me. I could see clearly that the difference between them and me - between them being dead and me being alive - was that I had at least somewhat of a warning. My Pa for one, and Jacob Snow and Cal too, warned me about such men and if it wasn't for that I wouldn't have made the sudden move to escape, and Jens' bullets would have hit their true marks, and I would have been shot dead.

There was a few minutes of silence after Rowdy told us about Antonio and Jens. Each of us was taking private stock of his or her own thoughts on the matter, and I reckon it was hard for all of us to come to grips with the truth of how evil a man can get.

Pa broke the silence when he said, "Jens sounds to me like a man in bad need of a noose around his neck, hanging down from a high, strong limb."

"That'd be a neat trick, Mr. McGee," Rowdy said, "If you could manage it. Might be a lot safer to shoot him off his horse from a distance with a nice fifty caliber Hawkins rifle."

"Next time I see Meesta Yens," Josefina snarled, "I will yus cut his corazon out of his chess." From somewhere in the folds of her petticoats she pulled out a long narrow knife and swung it in demonstration of what she would do to Jens. That Arkansas toothpick looked well honed and it put a little scare in me. I decided I better not ever forget that she had it hidden on her. Decided never to make her mad either.

It was clear that I wasn't the only person in the group who had been harboring thoughts of ill will against Jens, although I did feel my plans for him were quite a bit more sophisticated and included long periods of intense pain. But I decided I would allow Wind the final blow that would end his pathetic reign. For now I kept those thoughts to myself.

# CHAPTER THIRTY

*WIND'S NOSTRILS FLARED WIDE* and his eyes bulged with so much wild anger that white showed around the rims of them. Three big men were attempting to anchor the rope that was looped around his neck, but they were finding it an impossible task.

Wind walked on his hind feet, using his front hooves to strike at the offending rope around his neck. He recognized the men on the other end of the rope as the same ones who had earlier tried, unsuccessfully, to ride him. He hated the men and wanted only to be free of them and return to his owner.

The three men on the rope figured on  wearing the beast down until he had no energy left to fight them with. There was a fatal flaw in their figuring. They didn't know Wind. After a couple of hours the men got tired and gave up the struggle, and returned him to his reinforced box stall. That is, they flattered themselves that they put him in there.

The truth was that Wind returned himself to the stall, after a fairly good pretense at resisting of course. He preferred it to the mud hole they managed to create in the paddock outside of the stall. The cell was shaded and kept him cooler, without the sun beating down on his black coat. At least it used to be black. Before it got covered in mud and dust. Besides, he didn't want to see any part of the free world, including the sky.

The sky was the only thing visible from the paddock outside, other than the mud. They had erected a solid plank wall around it that was high enough to keep him from considering an attempt to jump over it. Why stare at the wide open skies when reaching it was an impossible goal. He'd rather hide in the shade of his cell.

# PART FOUR: THE GATHERING

A true bond, once forged, can be forgotten,
But can never be broken.

                    Doc Bonner

# CHAPTER THIRTY ONE

*AFRAID OF BEING DISCOVERED,* we agreed that we should leave camp at Frenchman's Ridge, which Rowdy informed us was the name of the small rise hiding our little valley from the trail. We planned to leave as soon as Rowdy and myself were able to travel more than just a few yards a day.

Jens figured me for dead, I was sure, or he wouldn't have left me there. But he could come looking for Josefina. She had not returned to work after her visit to the 'Chinese laundry'. She was certain that her boss would come looking for her, possibly alerting Jens to our presence in the process. Besides, we were in bad need of an easy source of food and supplies. And all agreed that a bath would be a wonderful thing as well.

It took another week for me to feel up to a full days travel. And just about as long for Rowdy to walk more than a dozen steps. During that period we discussed our future plans. We agreed that killing Jens was a primary desire. However, no matter how happy the idea made us, we debated the merits of the undertaking. At times we questioned the soundness of attempting to take him. He was a dangerous foe, and there was a chance that one or more of us could be killed in the attempt. I didn't care about the risk to my life, I only cared about one thing. Getting Wind back. I could scarcely think of anything else. Unless maybe it was Josefina.

In the end we decided that, for the sake of society, it would be worth the risk to go after him. After we decided to kill him, our palaver centered around how to go about it. We discussed the idea of involving the law, but soon had to forget about the idea. There was just no law to found in the region. Wyatt Earp might have been an effective ally against him but he was not a man for hire, and besides, rumors were that he left for California.

By the time we struck camp we had still not settled on a plan, but our relocation demanded full use of whatever wits we had left. So we quit arguing about how to best go about killing Jens and recovering Wind.

Our destination for a new home was a place that Rowdy knew of. It was one of Antonio's old spots. It was far enough away from Jens' range of crime that we could make our plans for Jens there, without having to watch our back so much. It had a small line cabin for shelter and Rowdy assured us that there was plenty of food and water.

Pa and Josefina each brought two horses with them, so we all had mounts to ride. But we were short one saddle. Rowdy still had his saddle. He had taken it off his horse just before turning it loose to fend on its own. My saddle was taken along with Wind. We decided to take turns riding bareback, except for Josefina of course.

We hit the trail early one morning and headed south. By noon I was done in but tried to hide it and continue on in spite of it. Josefina saw through me and called a halt. I had felt strong while doing nothing but sitting around camp, but hours on the trail was a different matter and I found out how weak I really had become. I don't think Rowdy felt much better than I did. He needed help from pa when he dismounted. The riding must have pained his leg plenty.

After resting, we rode on for another couple of hours before Pa told us we were camping for the night. We wanted to put more distance between us and Wichita that first day but there was no way I could go on, and Rowdy was looking pale.

We made a cold camp just in case anyone came close enough to smell a fire or see the light of one.

We struck out again early the next morning. I did a little better the second day but we still fell short of our hoped-for distance. Again we had to make due with a cold camp.

The next day we changed direction and started heading West. By the end of that day I had managed a few more miles than the previous two days, and could feel some of my strength coming back. Rowdy felt confident that we were no longer in Jens' territory so we had a fire in camp that night. Some color was back in Rowdy's face that night.

We were more relaxed that night and I enjoyed sitting by the fire with Josefina and my Pa, but I was quickly asleep. So far I had not taken a watch shift at night, the others had shared my shift. I felt bad about it, but knew I could never be trusted to stay awake. I vowed to make it up to them when I was able.

That night I dreamed of Wind, and woke in the morning with a terrible ache in my heart.

# CHAPTER THIRTY TWO

*"SHOOT THAT CRAZY SON OF A BITCH."* Jens growled. "I don't want to see him again, and I sure ain't wastin no more of our time on that mean excuse for a horse." He turned angrily on his heels and stomped back towards the saloon.

Rafael followed him, pleading for a favor. "Please senor, let me have him. If you don't want him no more I will take him. I will take him away from here, and deal with him on my own time."

"I said shoot him and I mean it. I only want to see him dead," Jens snarled, forgetting how great of a horse he had considered Wind to be a short time ago. "He has cost us too much trouble already. No one will ever be able to ride him. You've seen how he is. He's hopeless," Jens replied while stalking back into the bar.

"No Jefe, he is still useful. I can use him. You will see," Rafael pleaded some more.

"How the hell can you use a monster like that?" he demanded.

Rafael detected a tiny softening in Jens' defenses and he pushed on. "I can make money with him. I can charge monies for peoples to come see the monster loco horse. I will lock him in a big steel cage and he will be my own personal freak of nature."

Jens laughed at the thought. "Hell, Rafe, I think you're onto something there. That's the one thing that may be better than death for the idiot. Take him, he's yours. I hope you get rich off the freak." He laughed again and ordered a whiskey from Andrew.

# CHAPTER THIRTY THREE

*RILEY KNEW, WHEN SHAWN FIRST TOLD HIM* he was going to Wichita, what his reasons were, and it worried him then. It was plain to see that he was going for revenge. He didn't begrudge him his revenge, however. What angered and worried him was that he wouldn't let Riley come along to help him. Going up against a man with Jens' reputation might be a courageous thing to try, but Shawn might be getting himself into something he might not be able to get out of. Alive.

Now it had been more than two weeks since Shawn left for Wichita, and no word from him in the whole time. Riley decided it was time to quit worrying about him. He decided it was time to do something about it. He packed his horse and started traveling, ponying a spare mount behind.

He chose his horses for their endurance. One was a Morgan named Thor. He had a deep and narrow chest and never tired. Riley relied on him the most and he was in good condition, used to regular work. The spare was a paint horse he acquired recently named Wings. It was an apt name, he tended to be a bit flighty, as Riley had discovered. But he had a lot of bottom.

# CHAPTER THIRTY FOUR

*SHORTLY AFTER RETURNING HIMSELF TO HIS CELL*, Wind heard someone approaching. There were two men coming. When they got close to the paddock one of them was yelling angrily. It was the same man that had taken him from his owner. Then the other man spoke. Then the man who took him laughed and walked away. The other man said something. Then he left too.

The next morning Wind expected the men to show up again with the ropes and drag him into the mud, like they had on all the previous mornings. But no one showed up that morning, or the next one either. On the third morning he heard something approaching but was baffled by the sounds. They were not the usual voices of the men with the ropes. He heard the sound of wheels and a strange rattling sound that accompanied it. When the sound reached the edge of the paddock it stopped.

After a minute of silence he heard a human voice from just outside his cell. It spoke softly, the first time Wind had ever heard a soft spoken person since he was taken.

"You are very lucky," Rafael said quietly through the box stall wall, "Senor Jens wanted you killed. I saved you. And now you are mine."

Rafael didn't know if the horse could understand what he was saying, he figured he probably couldn't. But he knew he would understand what was happening to him soon enough.

Rafael made an opening in the paddock wall and then drove his special built new wagon through it. He backed the wagon up to the door of the box stall. The back of the wagon was very close to the wall of the stall, so that the horse inside could not fit between them.

He opened the stall door using the rope that the men left tied to the handle. The horse stood still, not wanting to walk in to the metal cage on the wagon. Rafael used a rope to slide a wooden ramp out the back of the wagon to make it easier for the horse to enter. But the horse still did not move. Rafael had anticipated the horses reluctance and had brought along a persuader.

He pulled a short ladder from the front of the wagon and leaned it against the wall of the stall. Then he took a grain sack from the wagon and carried it back to the ladder. The sack had something alive in it and appeared to move slightly.

He climbed up the ladder, to a twelve inch gap between the roof and the wall of the stall. He dumped the contents of the sack into the stall.

Rafael heard the rattles of the snakes first, then he heard the shrill shriek of the horse. After that there was much stomping of hooves, some snorting, more shrieking and a lot a banging against the walls of the stall.

Wind was truly terrified by the sudden appearance of several snakes writhing around between his legs. There was no way to escape them. Every step he took was no better than where his foot had just been standing. He tried banging himself against the walls, hoping they would give way and he could escape, but to no avial. He was hopelessly trapped with the snakes.

He heard a sound at the door to the cell. He looked towards it, desperately hoping that someone had come to take him out of his cell again. The strange metal door cracked open and his hopes soared. When it flew completely open,Wind lunged for it, not wanting to miss his chance for escape. He was all the way up the ramp before he realized what he'd done. He turned back but it was too late. A metal door was slammed shut and he was imprisoned in a new, and even smaller cell.

His new stall was built in a way that he could see all about him. The walls were not walls, they were thin metal bars. Like the kind he'd seen on stall windows and gates. He was confined, but at least he could see, and get plenty of air. But all around him the only thing he saw was the freedom of the open that he could never enjoy.

He flinched when he felt his new stall start to move. This was a sensation he had never experienced before. It felt similar to the train cars, but a lot rougher. He watched as his old cell disappeared in the distance, along with the town where the bad blond horse thief lived.

# CHAPTER THIRTY FIVE

*JOSEFINA WAS AT MY SIDE IN THE MORNING*, bringing me coffee and breakfast, like she did every morning. I smiled at her and my heartache eased a little. I still missed Wind terribly, but having Josefina made it almost bearable.

That day we traveled west, into some of the most remote country in the U.S., proving that Rowdy was correct when he told us that where we were headed we could count on never having to worry about receiving company. Not even Jens.

"How can you be so sure of that?" I asked. "If we can find it can't he find it too?"

"Only by some miracle," Rowdy replied. "That's how we found it the first time. Surely by the hand of God."

"What do you mean?" Pa asked him.

"I mean, one time a while back, me and the boys was trying to find water for a small herd of cattle we was deliverin up the trail. It was scarce and we was afraid of losing the herd if we didn't find some quick. It had been hot and dry for too long and all the regular waterin spots was dried up. Wasn't much hope of savin the cows, and then it got so's we was worried about savin our own selfs.

"We forgot about the cattle and went lookin for our own water. We had about gave up hope when Antonio started to sing. We thought he'd gone crazy from the thirst. He was singin an old church hymn called 'Walks on Water'. He was sorta driftin along while he sang, not going anywhere in particular. We all followed him, havin nothin better to do.

"Eventually all of us were singin the same song and driftin in the dry dust, not even lookin for water no more. We done give up, and was ridin to our final glory. Pretty soon I looked down and seen grass under our horses feet. Then I looked up and seen a big green valley stretched out in front of us, with a stream runnin right through it. We all seen it and stopped singin. We didn't talk, we just rode into the stream and watered up our horses and ourselves. An hour later the cows come draggin ass across the meadow and up to the stream."

111

"I'd call that a miracle," Pa said after a moment of silent thought.

"Is that where we are headed?" I asked.

"God willing," Rowdy replied.

# CHAPTER THIRTY SIX

*JUST BEFORE DUSK, ROWDY PULLED US UP.*
"This is where we lose our tracks," he said. "In case anyone tries to follow us. Watch where I ride and when I holler out for you, follow in my tracks single file."

He rode up the side of a small embankment that ended where a pile of big boulders came up against it. He rode about twenty feet, and then he seemed to disappear. Then we heard him call us to follow. I went next, keeping in his tracks.

I smiled when I realized what he did. From the other side of the boulders it appeared that there was a small avalanche of rocks that came down a narrow canyon and filled it up. But once you got to the other side, the canyon opened up again. You couldn't see it until you came up over the pile of rock. Anyone riding by would just assume it was a blocked canyon. The others came along behind me and they all chuckled when they discovered the opening.

"How did you ever find this?" Pa asked Rowdy, amazed.

"I told you, it was a miracle. None of us remember climbing over that embankment. We was ridin blind. Well not quite completely blind apparently," he answered. "Someone was watching for us. Maybe an angel."

Rowdy had one more chore to do. He got off his horse and limped back the way we had come in. He backed his way back in again, using a saddle blanket to wash out our tracks leading away from the main trail up the ridge. That erased the only sign which would indicate someone had veered off the trail. He was sweating and pale when he remounted, but still looked better than he had a few days earlier.

"After a few hours the wind will smooth out the little marks left by the blanket, and then no one can ever see a sign of travel there," he explained.

We rode on up the narrow canyon for several hundred yards, where it opened up suddenly into a wide green basin. It was just like Rowdy described it.

# CHAPTER THIRTY SEVEN

*RILEY AND HIS HORSES BOARDED A TRAIN* in St. Louis, for the
sake of saving time and horse flesh, just as Shawn had. He was in a
hurry, like Shawn, and wanted his horses in good shape when he
arrived in Wichita.

He had asked the conductor to stop the train a couple of miles
outside of Wichita and let him off early. It cost him an extra five bucks
to convince the conductor to do it, but it was worth it. He didn't want to
jump off the train in the main station, for all lookers to see. He wanted
to remain anonymous, and retain any advantage that surprise might
give him. You never knew.

After leaving the train he rode a little ways off of the main trail
leading into Wichita, but parallel to it, not wanting to meet someone on
the trail unexpectedly. He was wary and wanted to check out the people
and the town before they had the chance to learn about him. You can
learn a lot about the other players in a game by just watching and
listening. And if you stay in the shadows and keep your mouth shut you
get to know a lot more about them than they get to know about you.
Again, trying to keep any possible advantage he could.

As he rode he saw a strange looking wagon coming up the main trail,
away from the town. He rode further off the trail into some trees to gain
cover. He watched the wagon approach and as it got closer he noticed
that it had a sort of metal jail cell mounted in the back of it. Inside the
makeshift jail was a horse. He had never seen such a thing. He stared at
it as it got closer and closer, not believing his eyes. He could not figure
why on earth anyone would haul a horse in such a way.

When the wagon came as close to him as it was going to get he could
see the horse inside the cage clearly. It was in sorry shape. It was
coated in mud and god knows what else. It was wide eyed with fright,
but showing defiance at the same time. There was something about that
look in his eyes that reminded him of something, he thought he may
have seen that look before. He only had to ponder on it for a second
and he remembered where he'd seen it. It was in the eyes of the black

horse he gave Patrick when he left Richmond. Except this horse was not black, it was mud brown. Still he was sure that he would find a black coat under the mud.

He let the wagon go by and then slipped out of his cover and came back out on the main trail, behind the wagon. He rode up behind, slowly gaining on the wagon and studied the horse from a closer distance just to make sure he was right about it being the black. He was right.

He came around the wagon slowly until he was almost parallel to the driver, maybe a mite behind him.

"Howdy," he said loudly.

The driver flinched, surprised by the sudden appearance of Riley. The wagon he pulled was so noisy he never heard Riley coming. He swore at himself for not staying alert enough.

"Hello, senor," he said mildly, trying to hide his surprise. "Where you traveling?"

Riley ignored his question. "Unusual contraption you got on that wagon. What you got in mind with it?"

The drivers disposition changed a little. Not so sunny, Riley noticed. "Well now that's my own business is it not, senor," he said.

"Sure is," Riley said in a friendly tone. "Didn't mean to be rude, it's just that I ain't seen nothing like it before. Kinda got me curious."

Riley's friendly manner disarmed the driver a little and his features softened again.

"That's OK," the driver said, "I guess it is not no secret. I plan to show the horse to crowds of people. He's my meal ticket."

"How so?" Riley wondered.

"He's a loco horse. A monster. I will charge people to see a real monster," he explained. "Today you are lucky. You get to see him for free."

"Well thanks, mister. That's mighty kind of you," Riley said, continuing to gain his trust. "He must have cost you plenty, a horse that special."

"Not really. He was a gift," the driver explained.

"A gift you say. Now that's very generous. Maybe you should introduce me to the man. Maybe he will give me a horse too," Riley said in a half joking way, trying to build up the camaraderie.

The driver snorted a laugh and said, "I would not count on that. Jens is not the most generous man in the world. In fact he maybe is more likely to shoot you for asking," the driver said. "He only gave me this one because I work for him and he wanted to kill this horse anyway. I talked him into giving it to me instead."

"You work for him a long time?" Riley asked. He had already heard what he needed to hear. Jens' name. Now he wanted to find out just how involved this driver was.

"Yes," he answered. " I been with him many years now. He is a good man to work for."

That was enough information for Riley. Any man who would stay with Jens for a long time, and then consider him a good man, was a bad man himself. He knew how to handle this type.

"What's that over in the trees there?" Riley pointed in a direction away from himself.

The driver turned, afraid of what danger might be hiding in the trees. He never saw the danger riding next to him. Riley pulled his gun and shot the driver in the head. He would have aimed for the heart, that bein a better kill shot, but this man didn't have one.

Riley rode alongside the wagon team and pulled on the traces, stopping the wagon. He dismounted and approached the cage gently, trying not to spook the horse. It looked terrified so he spoke lowly and soothingly, trying to convey the idea that he was not a threat. After ten minutes of such talk the horse seemed to respond to him a little and looked a little less afraid, if still nervous.

Then Riley recalled that this black had been stable mates with his two horses, Thor and Wings, for a spell. He led his horses up to the cage and let them sniff at each other a while. The black seemed to recognize the other two horses and became a little more calm. Then Riley held his hand out for the black to smell.

The horse sniffed his hand a few times and then licked it, looking for food. He used to do that same thing every day at feeding time when Riley had him in Richmond. He decided the horse knew who he was. He got some grain out of his saddle bags and gave a handful to the horse, who ate it eagerly.

He wanted to put a bucket of water in the cage for him but it was too confined for the horse to reach it on the floor. Riley considered letting the poor horse out of the cage, but he knew it might not be as simple as he would wish.

The horse had obviously been through an ordeal, and was still a little spooked. Getting a halter on him may not be easy, if the horse didn't want to allow it. And if he let the horse out without some kind of control, there was a chance it would run off in terror and never be found again. But the horse couldn't stay in there forever so he had to try something, anything.

He slipped a halter through he bars of the cage and slowly raised it toward the horses nose, trying to get it on his head. The horse shied a little and Riley backed off just an inch or two. A minute later the black got calm again and the next time Riley slipped the halter up, the horse allowed him to put it on him. Next he tied a rope to the halter. Then he opened the door at the back of the cage.

At first the horse just stood there, afraid to move. Riley gave a little tug on the rope but the horse still wouldn't step back. Riley knew what was worryin the horse. The step down off the back of the wagon was pretty high. The black had no confidence in dealin with it. But Riley did.

He threw the dead body of the driver onto the other side of the bench on the wagon. Then he drove the wagon off the trail toward a shallow wash. The bank on the near side of the wash had been washed out and Riley drove the wagon into the bottom of the wash through this gap. He drove the wagon around the first bend in the wash, then stopped and backed the wagon up against the embankment on the other side. The bed of the wagon was just a little higher than the bank and it hung out over the top of it, a few inches above level ground.

He got out of the wagon and went to the back of the cage where he tugged on the rope tied to the horses halter. This time the horse backed out without a problem. It stood there for a minute, looking around to get it's bearings, then it nuzzled Riley's hand, looking for another handout.

# CHAPTER THIRTY EIGHT

*WHEN WE WERE DONE WITH ALL* the ooohs and the aaaahs, after seeing the beauty of the little canyon Rowdy brought us to, we watered the horses and ourselves and checked out the little cabin that was set up along the bench of the stream. It was only built for two cowboys to bunk in, and even that made a crowd, so we had to set up an additional camp. Josefina got the cabin of course, and I used up a lot of energy trying to think up a way to be able to share the small room with her. Nothing came to me right away but I didn't stop trying.

By the time we unpacked and settled in, it was almost dark. We got a fire going and cooked up some grub. Well, Josefina cooked it. I just watched her the whole time. Seems a lot of my time lately was spent watching her. I don't think she minded it though. A couple of times, when she caught me lookin at her, she gave a little smile.

After dinner we slept, tired after a hard ride. Bathing would wait one more day.

We didn't post a watch. Rowdy was convinced that no one could ever get here. I wasn't so sure. We were here weren't we? Antonio's bunch got here somehow, the first time they found it. Maybe it was miracle, but others have miracles too. What if another miracle happens to someone and they ride in here and surprise us? I considered that possibility for a while, then wondered if God would grant a miracle like that to an evil person. I didn't know. No one knew. And that's what worried me. But I was too tired to stand a watch so I figured I couldn't begrudge anyone else for not doin the same.

In the morning I woke up to the the smell of coffee, and the sight of Josefina making breakfast.

"Good morning, senor Patrick," she said with a smile. "Are ju hungry? We have beans and bread. Something different for the change." It was a little joke. We had been eating beans and hard bread for many days now.

"I'm starved," I replied.

"Me too," I heard pa say.

About that time Rowdy rode up to camp. He must have rode out early. I never even heard him leave, proving how tired I had been. Or how quiet Rowdy was.

"Yeah, me too," Rowdy said. "I'm ready for something different though. How 'bout beans and old bread, just for a change?"

The small grouped laughed and gathered around the fire to eat. After the meal was consumed we looked at each other, wondering who would start the conversation we all knew was waiting to be had.

"We all know that we got to make a real plan to deal with Jens," Rowdy started off evenly. "But before we get to that, I think we should do a little plannin for our situation here in camp. We need food, more wood, and some beds set up."

"Ok," pa said, "what do you suggest? This is your old grounds, so you know best."

"I know where to find the food, but I will need help with it," Rowdy responded. "Patrick ain't strong enough yet. You'll have to go with me, Shawn."

"What can I do?" I wondered.

"You can split wood and stack it for the fire. Just do as much as you can and then get rested up in between," Rowdy instructed. "And if you feel like it you can help Josefina clean out the cabin." I detected a funny smile when he said that.

I never saw more than a knee high piece of sage while riding into camp. I was doubtful that I would find enough wood to split, much less stack. Rowdy must have seen the question on my face.

"Don't worry," he said, "we brought in supplies of wood some time ago. Look behind the cabin," he finished with a broad smile.

Pa saddled up and they were ready to go hunting for meat. "See you tomorrow," Rowdy said with a wave as they were riding off.

Me and Josefina watched the two riders until they were out of sight. Then we stood and looked at each. Neither said anything to the other. The longing in our eyes seemed to be saying all that needed saying.

# CHAPTER THIRTY NINE

*RILEY UNHOOKED THE HORSES* from the harness of the wagon and set them free. He left the drivers body slumped on the bench of the wagon. He wasn't worth making the effort to bury. He pondered that decision a moment, realizing it was the action of a hard man not to bury someone proper. He wondered when he had become such a hard one as that. He'd had many rough experiences in his past. Experiences that he'd often thought no creature of God should be made to endure. Any one of them could have turned him to stone. He mounted up and ponied his two extra mounts back north, away from town.

His plan was to circle around Wichita to the East, then go south and come in from the opposite side of where he was now, the west side. By doing so he would avoid a few possible complications. He would be less suspect of involvement with the shooting of the wagon driver, in case his body was discovered soon. And he would not be suspected of having come from the train, making him appear more like he was part of a cattle drive. He wasn't sure what advantage that might give him but it was the only plan he had.

It was nearing dark by the time Riley and his horses completed their circumnavigation of Wichita and arrived some miles South of town. He circled west to intercept the main trail into town. Following a game trail he entered a low hidden valley, low ridges on either side. There was ample evidence that the canyon had been used as a camp recently. He reckoned it would do for a camp for the night and he dismounted. He led the horses down the slope and into the bottom of the valley.

As they approached the old fire ring the Black snorted and shied away. Riley could barely hold him. He had to let go of the lead of his other two horses to try to keep control of the Black. He saw fear in the horses eyes and it made him leery. Horses have better senses than humans and Riley had been wise enough to pay attention to his horses reactions more than once in his life.

"What's the matter boy," he said. He let the horse back up a ways, until it seemed to get a little calmer. Then he looked around, alert for anything dangerous. He stayed still and watched for a while but he didn't notice anything. No sounds. No smells. No predators.

He tied the Black to a tree several yards away from the center of camp. He seemed more calm there. Then, still cautious, he walked slowly into camp. He looked all about and saw several interesting things. There were old, blood soaked bandages on the ground. The ashes in the fire pit were deep. Someone had been here more than a week, and they were hurt. There were fresh tracks from four horses, and older ones for a few more.

He swore as he looked close at one set of tracks. They belonged to Shawn's horse. It was already too dark to follow the tracks. He would have to wait til morning.

He woke up early, anxious to track Shawn's horse. Hoping to catch up with him. Hoping he wasn't too late. The bloody bandages were a bad sign.

He looked over toward the Black, wanting to get him ready to travel, but the horse was gone.

# CHAPTER FORTY

*AFTER STARING AT JOSEFINA* for a minute or two she smiled and sat down next to the fire. I smiled too and sat next to her. There was a funny feeling between us, like being together was natural, and we felt a certain comfort with each other. But at the same time we were nervous and slightly embarrassed.

All kinds of things began stampeding through my mind. Thoughts about how I felt, about things I wanted to do, and about things I wanted to say. But my tongue was hog tied and I couldn't get a word out to save my life. Josefina didn't seem to have the same discomfort about speaking.

"I am glad that we are alone finally, senor Patrick," she said. If my mind had been under my control I could have read any number of things into what she meant by that statement. As it turned out I got lucky and said the right thing to her in return.

"Yeah, me too," I said. After I said it I was rewarded by Josefina with a wide, charming smile. That smile raised my spirits I guess, and my confidence rallied a little. I was able now to speak more than two words. They were words filled with hope.

"How should we take advantage of our time alone?" I asked.

"I want to tell ju about my plans for senor Jens. I was hoping that ju would help me convince the other two mens to do what it is I say," she told me.

"Oh," I said. I tried to hide my disappointment, but I must have failed miserably. Josefina's face fell, and her smile faded.

"Ju were expecting something else, senor Patrick?" she asked with a small frown.

I ignored her question, for now. "I wish you would call me Patrick. Calling me senor makes me feel sorta like you were my servant or something. I want you to be my friend, not my servant."

"Ok, Patrick," she said. "I want to be ju friend too."

"Is that all you want to be Josefina, my friend?" I asked her. I noticed my hands were sweating again. It had been a long time since that had happened. I was frightened. Not by the dangers of a murderer, but by a woman. By the chance she might not want me.

"I am afraid senor. I mean Patrick," she said. I had never considered that possibility before. She never acted afraid. She always seemed so confident.

"What are you afraid of?" I asked her. If she was afraid of the same thing I was afraid of I would be a very happy man. I could only hope.

"Many things I am ascared for," she said. "I am ascared about Jens and what happen if ju do not kills him when ju try. If ju no can kill him, he will kill ju. And I am ascared of what happen if ju kills him. Maybe ju will be arrested and go to prison forever. And I am ascared of ju going to ju home with ju padre after we kills senor Jens."

I realized that everything she feared came down to the same one thing. She was afraid of losing me. She was afraid of the same thing I was afraid of, us not being together.

Now, several months ago, back in Richmond, I would have been terrified at the prospect of having a woman care for me so deeply. Given the same circumstances I now faced with Josefina I would have stood up and bolted like a frightened deer. But I suppose that I had done a little growing up, and was no longer a frightened animal.

Without realizin what I was about to do I leaned over toward her and put my hand around the back of her head. Then I pulled her toward me and kissed her. I've got to admit it probably wasn't much of a kiss. I wasn't really all that experienced at kissing, having done little of it in my past. In truth I guess I'd never done any kissing in my past. None of this kind of kissing anyway. But nonetheless it had the desired, if unexpected, effect on both of us.

I pulled back from her, my lips on fire, and looked in her eyes, not really knowing what to expect. I saw in her eyes the same thing I felt in my heart and I knew at that moment I was lost.

We stared at each in a sort of delicate rapture for a very long time. At least I *think* it was a long time, but to be honest I have no idea how long it was. Anyway, at some point she took my hand and walked toward the cabin. I followed willingly of course. Like I said earlier, I might have been a coward but I was no idiot.

It was dark when we came out of the cabin again, and I am not sure it was any cleaner when we left it than it was when we entered it. What I am sure of is that I was not the same person coming out that I was going in.

I split some wood and got a fire going while Josefina prepared some food and coffee for us. After the meal we sat by the fire with our arms around each other. I think it was at that moment that my life took another big turn and stepped out onto a solid wide path that would guide the rest of my future.

We talked some while sitting by the fire, but mostly we didn't have much need to speak. Just being together was enough.

# CHAPTER FORTY ONE

*THE NEXT MORNING, JUST BEFORE SUNUP*, we heard riders approach the cabin. We dressed quickly and went outside. It seemed we didn't dress quickly enough and when we got outside Pa and Rowdy were already in camp. Rowdy looked at us with a sly smile but was man enough not to say anything, yet. Pa frowned a little, but like Rowdy he didn't say anything.

I looked at the small packets of meat they had untied from their horses and said, "Is that all you got?" It came out different than I meant it and I regretted saying it. But Rowdy didn't seem to take it the wrong way.

He said, "No, we got a whole lot more stashed yonder. And since it looks like you done healed up real quick, I reckon you can take a pack horse with you and retrieve it for us." Then he laughed, but it was a friendly laugh.

"Me an you will go together," Pa said, "I'll show you the way. But first we eat some of this here meat for breakfast. For a *real* change in the menu. Then we'll get a couple of horses ready and head out after the rest of the meat." Then, unable to resist ribbin me like Rowdy done, he said, "You're up to it ain't ya?" And he laughed too.

I didn't take offense to the ribbing. I could tell that they were happy about seeing me walk out of Josefina's cabin when they rode up. They were just using the joking as a way to let me know that they had no objection.

After we finished with the delicious breakfast of fresh meat, Pa and I left camp. The meat wasn't too far off and I was surprised when I saw the huge pile of it, all wrapped up neat in a hide. The hides looked like buffalo to me and I wondered where they found one.

"Now I see why you couldn't bring it all in at once," I said. "I didn't know there was any buffalo left in these parts," I added.

"Neither did I, " Pa said, "Rowdy knew of another secret spot nearby. A small herd manages to forage and escape detection there."

We packed all the meat up on our horses and hauled it back to camp. Rowdy had lifted a trap door in the ground near the bank of the stream. There was a cellar dug into the ground there that was cool enough to preserve the meat just long enough to give us time to dry it and prepare it. We were putting the last of the meat in the cellar when I heard Rowdy drop his load of meat and draw his gun. He hit the dirt while warning us to get down.

I laid low and heard the sound of a horse coming towards us. I drew my gun and looked around for Josefina, hoping she was under safe cover. Pa pointed to the cellar, indicating to me that Josefina was in it. I nodded my understanding, and my thanks.

We all waited, hearts racing, senses alert. The hooves approached slowly and when they got within a dozen yards they stopped. We couldn't see the horse from our hiding spots, we could only hear it. After several minutes the rider of the horse hadn't spoken.

"If you be a friend, come in slow with your hands where we can see em and declare yourself," Rowdy hollered. He rolled to a different spot as soon as he finished, just in case the intruder took a shot at the direction of his voice.

After several more minutes there was still no response. The only sound was an occasional sound of a horse blowing, or a low knicker. Then I heard a low whinny.

As soon as I heard it I got up and walked out in its direction. I'd know that whinny anywhere. Pa tried to warn me back but I kept going.

"Well I'll be damned," I said when I got a look at the horse. It was Wind.

The minute he saw me he walked up to me. I scratched him on his chin, knowing its what he likes, and he sniffed at my hand, looking for grain.

The others, not hearing any shooting or fighting, came out from their cover and looked on with amazement. I didn't even care if they saw my tears I was so happy.

Josefina ran up and hugged both of us at the same time.

It was true that Wind was a sight for sore eyes, but he was a sorry sight for sure. He looked like he'd been through hell. He was brown instead of black and he stunk to high heaven. He had lost a lot of weight too, and had several bare patches on his hide from various cuts and scrapes.

We took him to the stream and washed him while he was drinking. When he was done drinking we gave him a little grain, but not too much, then turned him out on the grass. While he was eating we all took turns guessing about what had happened to him during his absence, and how he had found us.

I was extremely pleased to have Wind back again, and I watched him all through the day. That night while I slept in the cabin, with Josefina, I dreamed repeatedly about him.

The next morning I bolted out of the cabin as soon as I awoke, worried that he might have disappeared again. But he was still there and I went back inside and got dressed proper.

After breakfast Pa took me aside and said, "It's time for you to practice up with your gun. We are all going to have to be damn proficient with our firearms if we want a chance against Jens."

We walked downstream to a spot where there was a low bank of dirt that we could shoot against. We set up some various items from around camp to use as targets. Pa took me about ten paces back from the targets and we started shooting. He gave me lot of pointers and I practiced on what he told me to do. We practiced til lunch and took a break to eat. Then we started practicing again.

A few hours later my hand was sore and my ears were ringing and I was tired. I never would have figured that shooting a gun could be so hard on a body. I told Pa it was time to quit for the day. As we walked back to camp we heard Rowdy shout.

"Rider comin," he hollered.

We all dove for cover again, and I wished my hand wasn't so tired from practicing. Now is when I might need a steady hand.

This time we didn't have to wait out the suspense of who it was.

"Hello the camp," a familiar voice rang out.

"Well I'll be damned," Pa said and left his cover to go greet the man.

Following Pa's lead we all came out from cover and tagged along behind him. I recognized the newcomer at once of course, although Rowdy or Josefina wouldn't know him. It was the rude stable man, Riley.

"Howdy, Shawn," Riley said as he dismounted. "I see yon Patrick there is not quite as dead as the rumors would have him." He shook Shawn's hand and patted him on the shoulder.

"Right you are, Riley," Pa said. "Your senses are as keen as ever."

"And I see he found that gun you left in his bags as well," Riley said.

"Right you are again, Riley. Now come to the fire and eat. We will take care of your horses."

Riley approached me with his hand offered to me for a handshake. I took his hand gladly. This was the man that insisted I take Wind, when I thought I wanted a different horse. He was a man who knew the difficulties I would be facing when I rode west out of Richmond. A man who cared enough about my success to insist on me taking Wind. And now, here he was, a long way from home trying once more to look out for me and Pa.

"I'm damn happy to see you, Riley," I said while gripping his hand firmly. "I can't thank you enough for giving Wind to me. He saved me more than once, that's for sure."

"If you are talkin about that black horse I gave you you are very welcome. Wind would be a fitting name for him too," he said. Then he added, "You still sore at me for what I done in the stable in Richmond?"

"Naw," I said. "Not any more. I was for the first two miles after I left, but then the only thing that was sore after that was my butt." I smiled and Riley smiled back, everything forgiven and forgotten between us. Then Riley stopped smilin and his face turned a bit serious and he turned away to get some grub by the fire.

We all sat around the fire watching Riley eat. When he was done he said, "I thought all of you were likely dead by now."

# CHAPTER FORTY TWO

*RILEY HAD FOLLOWED WINDS TRACKS* into our camp, otherwise he would never have found us. Rowdy had to go back to the turn off from the main trail and erase the tracks again. He had just returned when he heard Pa's response to Riley's fear of our being dead.

"Lucky for us you are wrong," Pa said.

"I agree," Riley said. Then he pulled a bottle out of his saddlebags and passed it across to Shawn. "Let's drink to your fortunate resurrection," he said.

"You brought this all the way from Richmond," Pa asked, holding the bottle out.

"No sane Irishman leaves home without his whiskey. For emergencies don't ya know," he explained.

"I didn't bring one with me," Pa said.

"Like I said, no *sane* Irishman would do it," he clarified.

Pa just grunted and handed the bottle around.

For the rest of the night we passed the bottle around and I told Riley all about what had happened to me since I left. And he, in turn told us about his trip, and running into Wind in the cage, and what the man who had caged him said about his intentions for him. He seemed proud of his confession that he had 'dispatched the mans black soul'.

I had a hard time accepting that Riley downright murdered that man with no hesitation and with no regrets. I wondered about it for a while, trying to decide if he could be one of the evil men Pa warned me about. It didn't add up, so I left it alone for a later time.

When we finished our stories Riley looked over at Josefina, who was sitting close up next to me. He seemed to be thinking, putting some pieces together, while watching her.

"You the Josefina who sent the telegram announcing Patrick's murder?" he asked her.

"Jes, senor. I send it to senor Shawn when I hear the news in town. Then I go to find Patrick's body and make it buried properly. But his body no dead. Yus shot up. We think for while maybe he still going to die. I am glad he did not." She turned and smiled at me.

Riley nodded and smiled but said nothing, understanding, now, our attachment to each other.

For some time no one spoke. There was a quiet reflection taking place in all of us as we stared into the flames of the fire. We were all reflecting on the same thing, afraid but yet determined.

It was Riley who finally brought it out in the open. "Seems that the only thing that remains to be done now is to figure out a way to rid the country of a plague called Jens. He said it like it was a simple matter for him to decide on the good or the evil, the right or the wrong of a man, and once he determined which it was, he had no further reservations on the matter. Wasn't that simple or easy for me.

"In the morning," Pa said.

# CHAPTER FORTY THREE

*THE NEXT MORNING I WOKE UP IN THE CABIN*, wrapped close around Josefina. I heard others, outside, already moving about. I knew I should get up and help with whatever needed done, but I wasn't able to extract myself from her.

As if reading my mind, Josefina stirred and turned to face me.

"We have to get up now, Patrick," she said.

Reluctantly I got out of bed and pulled on my boots. Josefina got dressed hurriedly, wanting to fix breakfast for us. I heard her greet the others after she left the cabin, and I hesitated to follow behind her.

I knew what we had planned for the day, and I was not as sure about it as I was a few days ago. I had begun to lose my interest in killing Jens right after I spent my first day with Josefina, in the cabin. Then after Wind came back to me I lost even more interest. Now I had grave doubts about what I really wanted concerning him.

I finally left the cabin after Josefina called for me, telling me breakfast was ready.

After breakfast was consumed we gathered around the fire, ready to make our plans for Jens. I had decided while eating that I was going to make my feelings known right off.

"I'm not so sure any more that we really need to kill Jens," I announced.

There was silence for a moment and then Pa said, "I understand your reluctance son. None of us looks forward to the task. We all wish it didn't fall on us to have to do something about the man. But there is a funny thing that happens when you gain knowledge of something. Along with that knowledge comes a responsibility. Once you know for sure that there is something that needs fixin, you are bound to the duty. If you turn your back on it, you turn your back on yourself, on your own honor, and you die a little. You invite a little misery into your life. And that's not mentioning the effects it might have on others who could be harmed if you don't fix whatever it is you see needs fixin.

"Like I said," Pa continued, "None of us likes what we got roped into, but we did. Now its up to us to do something about it. We can't hope that someone else will do it. Who else is there? Besides, no one else has done anything about it so far. Just think, if they did you wouldn't have been shot. And worse, you could easily have been killed. How are you going to feel about the next innocent person Jens kills, knowing that maybe you could have prevented it?

"It ain't an easy thing, it takes real courage. Real grit. But I know we all got the sand to go through with it. Afraid or not, we'll do what's right, even if it is because we are more afraid of what will happen to our souls if we turn our back on it."

I hadn't been looking at it quite that way. I had only been thinkin about my own personal reasons. I lost my desire for revenge because I got Wind back and now I had Josefina. But Pa was right, there were more important reasons for stopping Jens.

"I see your point, Pa," I said to him.

## PART FIVE – THE RECKONING

Revenge is not considered a human virtue,
Yet mankind puts an uncanny value on justice.

Doc Bonner

# CHAPTER FORTY FOUR

*"LET'S MAKE US A PLAN,"* Riley said, getting down to business.

We all circled around the campfire with our best conspirator's attitude, serious faced and bent forward. I glanced at Josefina, wondering if she was still of a mind to put forth her plan. And if so, was I still expected to back her on it.

She didn't speak up, and she didn't give me any little clues that she still had the inclination to convince the others of a superior plan. I wondered if what she said about it the day before wasn't just a way of tellin me she worried about me.

Pa was the first to put forth an idea, just as I expected he might be.

"I think we can all agree that Jens is a worthy adversary," he started. "I suggest we start out here by discussing all the things we admire about him."

Rowdy and Josefina both jumped to their feet at the same time. Rowdy opened his mouth as if to speak but apparently was unable to. Josefina had no problem speaking.

"Ju are loco mister," she said rather loudly, and almost hysterically. "The only thing I will ever admire about Jens is how much I like seeing his corazon stuck to the earths by my knife."

Pa held his hands up, palms out, trying to calm them down and to get a chance to explain himself. Rowdy remained standing and glaring at Pa but indicated he would give Pa the chance he wanted. Josefina muttered non-stop under her breath, and I was glad I couldn't understand Spanish.

Pa spoke again, ignoring Josefina's mutterings. "It's not how it sounds. I have my reasons for what I said and I think they are good ones. Please hear me out," he pleaded.

"I think you best be makin sense real quick," Rowdy commented.

"We'll never be able to come up with a safe plan until we face our demon," Pa started. "And I mean really face him, not just hate him. We have to back up from our hate for a minute because it blinds us. And a blind fighter is a dead fighter." He paused for a second and I noticed Rowdy getting a little calmer, but still standing. Josefina stopped muttering and started listening, even if still skeptical.

"I know it's hard," he continued. "How do you think I feel. He almost killed my only son. I left Richmond to come after him, driven only by hatred. I ate it, breathed it, let my heart pump it through my veins and define my existence. I let it blind me to all but the death of Jens. And I am very lucky I did not get the chance to face him before I found Patrick alive, or I would very probably be dead right now. I was crazy with hate, in no condition to face a foe as savvy as him. He would have kilt me, I'm sure of it."

He paused again, lost in thought, or memory, for a moment. Rowdy and Josefina had both sat back down and were considering what Pa had said.

"Then what's our reason for killing him," I asked, "if it's not because we hate him?"

"It's OK to have that reason, if that's what it takes to give you the desire to kill him. I ain't sayin you can't never hate him," Pa explained. "It's just that we need to be smarter than him if we want to overcome him. Make no mistake, he's a very shrewd man. He has to be to stay alive, unchallenged, for as long as he has. You ever wonder why no one has faced him down yet? It's not because he is more evil than anyone else, or more mean, or a better shot, or anything like that. It's because he is so smart. He's a thinker, and he always outfoxes anyone who tries for him. People who know that about him start to think they aren't up to the task of winning against him, so they don't try. And they are alive today for making that decision.

"So like I said, we better not lie to ourselves about him. We better fall in love with the man for a few minutes if that's what it takes for us to be objective about this mess." He stopped, waiting to see how we would take what he'd said so far.

I think we all started to figure out his reasoning, and we sure didn't feel like getting killed in process of killing Jens, so we paid attention to what he said.

"I think you are gettin through to us Shawn," Riley said, "But just what is it we should do, besides pretending he's a hero or something?"

"Let's just take an honest look at his real strengths and abilities," Shawn replied. "Once we do that, I think we are going to be surprised to realize exactly what lengths we will have to go to in order to succeed in killing him. Especially without all or most of us dying in the process."

"Ok, that makes sense to me," Riley said. "Where do we start?"

"We start with Rowdy," Pa said, "He has the most experience with the man."

All eyes turned to Rowdy who said, "Most of what I know is from stories I heard. Most of them was from Antonio, who knows him about as good as anyone I suppose. My own personal experience with him ended badly. I was lucky to escape with my life.

"I think," Rowdy continued, "I learned the most about him, though, in our most recent meeting, when his men ambushed us. I remember being surprised at how well he had out planned us. We thought we knew what he was gonna do. Even Antonio thought he had him figured out. That's what I remember thinking when the ambush hit us. I thought how Antonio was wrong about Jens."

"Ok," Pa said. "So that's another example of how smart he is. He can out-fox others. Anyone want to add to what Rowdy said?" he asked.

"He is a sneaky," Josefina said. "He tell you one thing, and do some other thing. And he get his men to do things for him, so he not in no danger. But I think the mos ascary thing of him is I think he not from the Earth."

We all looked at each other after hearing that, wondering if one of us understood what she meant, but none of us did.

"What does that mean, Josefina," I asked her. "That part about not from the Earth?"

"I mean he is maybe part demon. Something no natural," she explained.

I was still a little confused, and I could see the others were just as mystified as I was.

"What makes you say that?" I asked.

"I think he can know what ju are thinking in jor mind, then he is ready for what it is ju doing," she explained.

"That's interesting," Pa said. "I've heard about things like that. We used to hear stories about people like that in the old country. Remember that, Riley?"

"Yes, I do. I think they called them seers, or something like that. It would explain a lot about Jens if he was one of them. Explains how he's managed to survive so long," Riley answered.

"I remember something Antonio once said about him," Rowdy said. "He said that Jens avoided using a routine. He never did something more than once, or in the same way twice. Like he always took rustled cattle to a new spot, by a different trail. Never rustled from the same outfit more than once. Never used the same hide out more than once, especially after he was found in the one he thought Antonio had betrayed."

I listened to what the others were saying, hoping I could come up with something of my own to contribute, but I just drew blanks. Whenever I thought of him, all I could see was him sitting on his horse with a gun pointed at me, and then pulling the trigger. Over and over in my mind I replayed the explosion of the gun and the simultaneous impact of the bullet on my body. I just could not see anything smart or special about it.

After many minutes of replaying the shooting in my head, I recalled something that I had forgotten all about til now. I recalled that one of Jens men came into camp from the other side of the canyon. He'd sneaked up behind me without me hearing him, and I'd been surprised by that. I realized now that they knew the area well, and they knew I would be there, somehow. I mentioned it to the others, then Riley came up with a plan.

# CHAPTER FORTY FIVE

*"I THINK I HAVE AN IDEA,"* Riley said. He waited for a response but no one said anything. They just looked at him, waiting for the plan.

"Jens doesn't know me," he continued. "He's never seen me and probably never heard of me. I believe we can set a trap for him, using one of you for bait, and I can be the one to draw him out, into the trap."

For the rest of the night we listened to Riley lay out his plan. We asked a lot of questions and voiced various objections or worries about some aspects of it, and then came up with solutions and, over the space of several hours, we perfected the plan. Then we repeated it over and over until we all knew it cold.

When it grew late, and we all grew tired, Josefina and I went to the cabin and the others bunked down outside. We laid next to each other in the dark and spoke in whispers for a long time before sleep took us. We spoke of the plan and our fears of what it would mean if we failed. We spoke of our feelings for each other, as if realizing the possibility that we might not get another chance to express them.

Our love for each other deepened, reaching a new level, after our conversation that night. In the morning, when we awoke, we clung to each other for some time. We were reluctant to release our grip on one another, our strengthening bond driven by the dire outlook in our future.

We finally let go of each other, got dressed and joined the others. Josefina made breakfast and we ate in silence. The mood was somber, gloomy thoughts about the task ahead of us pushing us into dark reflections.

# CHAPTER FORTY SIX

*"HOWDY STRANGER," ANDREW SAID*, "what can I get you?" The Wichita barkeep of the Cattleman's Saloon had a policy of being friendly with new people, hoping for their repeat business.

"Whiskey please," Riley told him. He'd rode in early in the day. He was all dusty and looking like a regular cow puncher. It was not quite noon when he entered the Cattleman's Saloon. A carefully calculated time.

Andrew delivered the shot and Riley paid him. He wasted no time disposing of the shot and before Andrew moved the bottle very far away he ordered another. He disposed of that shot in the same manner and ordered another. All also carefully calculated.

"Why don't I just leave the bottle," Andrew said, not wanting to stand there pouring shots for the man all day.

"Why don't ya," Riley said.

Andrew set the bottle down, picked up the dollar Riley paid him for it, and strode a ways down the bar. He began washing glasses, but kept a close eye on Riley while doing so. Riley was pleased to see the suspicions in his eyes, it was what he had hoped for. So far the plan was going as expected.

Riley took a minute to glance around the room, trying not to be too apparent. Jens was there, at the poker table with what looked like a few of his men.

A few minutes later Andrew came back down the bar and approached him. He eyed the half empty bottle.

"Kinda early in the day for such heavy drinkin," Andrew said to Riley.

"What do you care," Riley responded, "I paid for it didn't I?"

"You sure did," Andrew said. "Didn't mean nothing by it, just wondered if you was in some kind of trouble is all. Usually this kind of drinkin means trouble of some kind. Maybe I can help that's all."

Andrew was beginning to fall neatly into Riley's trap. Good thing too, if he'd had to drink the whole bottle he may have passed out before having a chance to continue with the plan.

"Naw, no trouble. Not any more anyways. She was a whore to start with. Who needs her," Riley said, starting to slur a little. "To hell with ol' Josefina, that's what I say."

Andrew flinched, just a little, then squinted slightly. "You say Josefina, mister?"

"Yes I did," Riley answered. "I said to hell with her." He poured another shot for emphasis. He was pleased to see the wheels spinnin in Andrew's head, just as planned.

"What does this Josefina look like," Andrew asked, trying to sound nonchalant.

"She looks like a Mexican whore, that's what she looks like," Riley said with an increasing slur.

Andrew proceeded to give Riley a description of Josefina and then asked him if it wasn't what his gal looked like.

"Yep, that's the whore," Riley said. "I see she gets around some, just like a whore." He weaved a little and then poured another shot. He was pretending, partly, to be a little blind from drink, but he carefully noted that Andrew was swallowing the bait.

"You seen her near here somewheres did you?" Andrew asked, swallowing a bit further.

"You ain't a kiddin," he said loudly, hoping Jens would hear. "I seen her alright. Seen her with that asshole Patrick McGee. If I ever see him again I aim to shoot him." Pretending to be losing control of himself from likker he turned his head around the room, not focusing on anything in particular. But he got a quick enough look at Jens to know that what he had just said had gotten his attention.

Andrew noticed Jens' interest as well and he backed off down the bar again. Riley pretended to be unable to stand up steady and found a chair and table to sit at, choosing one sort of close to Jens table.

A moment later Jens turned his chair a little, so he could face toward Riley. He had a big smile on his face that made Riley's blood run cold, and he began to have an appreciation for why Jens had such a terrifying reputation.

## CHAPTER FORTY SEVEN

*WE LEFT THE REMOTE VALLEY* the morning after making our plan. We rode for two days, until we reached a small coulee near a stream and made camp, thus establishing our new base of operation. The coulee had good shade, provided by some cottonwood trees and plenty of water. More importantly it was less than a days ride from Wichita, an important factor if our plan was to work.

It was the first time I rode Wind further than a half mile since he came back to us, and it felt wonderful to have him with me again. Except for being a little scratched up he was just as fit and grand as he was before Jens took him.

The first night in camp we reviewed our plan and bedded down early. At first light we were up and bidding good luck to Riley. He rode off to Wichita to carry out the first steps of our plan.

After he left I turned to Josefina and said, "I still don't like it."

She smiled at me and said, "I love ju too, Patrick. But we talk enough about it before, and we already say there is no one else."

"I know," I said, "but it don't mean I have to like it."

"So ju hab said one thousand times," she said.

"And I will say it another thousand times too," I said, "or until Jens is dead, whichever comes first."

"Then we better kill him fast," Pa said, overhearing us. "Because I don't think I could stand to hear you say it one more time. Here," he continued, handing me an ax, "make yourself useful and start cutting some firewood."

While I cut wood, Josefina unpacked more supplies and stretched a tarp over a rope we had stretched between two of the cottonwoods, making a crude shelter. Then she checked on the horses. We had them tethered to a line we had stretched between two other cottonwoods, not far from our main camp. Josefina gave them a little more grain. Wanting them to be in good shape when needed.

After cutting a good sized pile of firewood we gathered some large rocks and built a fire ring with them. We got a fire going in it and kept it blazing. A few feet back from the fire Josefina laid out our sugguns

141

all in a row. On the opposite side of the fire we rolled some stumps into place for use as stools.

While we were setting up these items we made sure to leave lots of visible tracks going in and out of camp. At the end of the day we moved the whole camp, except for the fire ring and pile of firewood. We fed the fire to keep it going.

# CHAPTER FORTY EIGHT

*RILEY WAS HAVING A LITTLE TROUBLE SPEAKING* in a way that others might understand, but he'd been drunker than this before and still managed. He could do it again now. Especially now that he had a strong reason.

"Sorry, stranger but I couldn't help hearin you mention wantin to shoot a fellow a moment ago," Jens said to Riley with an evil grin.

"You mean Patchrick?" he slurred. "Damn right, I aim to shoot the shkunk next time I see him, and the whore too."

"Maybe we can help each other," Jens suggested.

"How you figger, mishter," Riley barely managed to say.

"It just so happens that he betrayed me too," Jens lied. "I been lookin for him. Lookin for my chance to get even if you know what I mean." In truth the only thing Jens looked forward to was finishing what he started. Namely killing Patrick. He had even more reason to kill him now than he did before. Now Patrick was potentially capable of testifying to being shot by him. Something Riley already knew and was counting on.

"Corsh I know what you mean," Riley said as if annoyed by Jens question. "But I don nee no hel," he managed, then hiccuped.

Jens turned his chair toward Riley a little further and his smile got a lot meaner. Riley realized he had pushed it far enough. Now all he had to do was set the hook.

"Maybe a lil bit hel," Riley admitted, "Never know what a lousy snake like tha ki wil do. But I'm bosh of this her deal, got it?" he said menacingly. This was the dangerous part, but he had to get at the man's pride in order to get him fully committed.

Jens rose from his chair with an expression Riley never wanted to see on any mans face again. "I'll be dead and rotting in hell and still never take orders from a drunkard like you, mister." Then he reached for the butt of his gun and said, "Got it?"

Riley got it. He had no doubt that Jens would shoot him dead right here and now.

"Guess yur rit," he said. "Probly be too drunk to fin my way to ther camp anyhow."

"They have a camp?" Jens asked.

"Shur they do. Thas war I sheen em. All lovy dovy." Riley knew he had him now. So far the plan was proceeding like it was supposed to. He just hoped the others were ready.

Jens strode over to Riley, aiming to force his point completely home. He sneered as he drew his ham-like fist back and then punched the drunk and drooping Riley in the jaw so hard in knocked him off the chair and rolled him several feet across the floor. Riley was stunned him to the point of seeing stars. He came close to blacking out but managed to regain his senses. The ordeal had the side effect making him a bit more sober. He started to rise from the floor but Jens was still standing over him looking threatening. Riley didn't stand a chance against him so he laid back on the floor.

"Get up," Jens ordered him. "I ain't gonna hit you again. I need you sober, drink some coffee. Andrew, get him some coffee. And be quick." He sat back in his chair and Riley warily rose up off the floor and returned to his chair. Neither man spoke. Riley avoided looking at Jens, but he could feel his steely eyes boring into him. When Andrew brought the coffee to him it was a welcome distraction.

"Thanks," Riley mumbled. His jaw was swollen and he had a hard time moving it without feeling a shooting pain. It was broken, but he found himself thinking that he was lucky that was all the damage he'd incurred. He sipped his coffee for a while and began gathering a few more of his wits about him. After he finished the mug of coffee Jens spoke up again.

"You sober enough to ride now?" he asked Riley.

"Might need one more cup," Riley answered. While it was true that he could use another mug, he was also thinking about the others and wanted to give them as much time as he could to get in position and be prepared.

"You sound sober to me," Jens said. "Let's go get that Patrick dude before they leave camp and skip out of the country." He stood up and came to Riley, lifting him off the chair by his arm. It took little effort for him to lift Riley, who wasn't a lightweight. Experiencing Jens unnatural strength added another level of respect, and fear, of the man. He wondered if Josefina wasn't right after all. Maybe Jens was not from this Earth.

Riley followed Jens out of the saloon and they caught up their horses. Four of Jens' men came along as well. One rode on either side of Riley and watched him closely. The other two rode behind, just in case Riley slipped by the two beside him. That's when it dawned on Riley that Jens never intended for Riley to return from this excursion alive, and he felt the cloak of death brush against him.

He'd felt the hand of death before and was familiar with its touch. The first time was as a boy back in the old country, when Shawn had intervened at the last second before his doom. He'd survived every skirmish he'd had with death so far. But that fact didn't encourage him right now because, in his mind, it had always been sheer luck that saved him. Every previous time that he'd been in death's grasp he had given in to it, and accepted the truth of its conquest. Never once had he reasoned that if he'd cheated death once, he could do it again, he'd had always and only experienced the concept of surrender.

Jens spoke again just after leaving town limits, causing Riley to stop wondering who, or who not, might be attending his funeral. "Tell us where the camp is," he ordered.

"I hope I can recall," Riley said, frowning.

Jens stopped his horse and rode up close to Riley with his hand on the handle of his gun. His meaning was clear and Riley had a sudden recollection. Of course he had never really forgotten, but was only trying to give his friends more time to execute their end of the plan.

"Ok, I remember now," he said quickly. "Its this way." He pointed off to the Southwest. "Follow me," he instructed.

"Hold on there," Jens said. "You point the way and I will lead. You stay behind me."

"Whatever you say,"Riley said. He'd rather not have a killer like Jens at his back anyway.

They rode along with Riley giving occasional directions, but the trail was fairly clear and they traveled the distance with no troubles.

When they got to the camp Riley said, "This is it. This is where I saw the whore and the asshole, Patrick." It was obvious that the camp was deserted. Riley worried that Jens would blame him for it and shoot him out of anger, so he watched Jens carefully.

Jens dismounted and examined the camp. He felt the ashes in the fire and then checked the horse droppings and other sign. He came up with the proper conclusion, which verified the accuracy of Riley's story, saving him from being shot.

"They were here," Jens said to him men. "And not long ago. Follow the tracks and let's chase em down."

His men didn't have much trouble finding the clear signs intentionally left by the avengers as part of their plan. The next few minutes would prove the worth of their plan.

# CHAPTER FORTY NINE

*RILEY WAS THANKFUL TO JENS* for one thing anyway, the coffee. He was not as drunk as he might have been otherwise and in the next few minutes it was vital that he have as clear of a head as possible. He was also thankful that Jens or his men did not search him. Otherwise they might have found the guns he had hidden under his clothing.

He followed Jens' men while two more followed behind him. He reached carefully under his garments, getting a grip on his gun. He held it there, not wanting to expose it yet.

As they started up Frenchman's Ridge, Jens seemed to realize that he was in a place he had been before. A sly smile showed on his face and he spoke to his men.

"I thought I kilt that bastard, Patrick last time we was here. Now I get to do it again. Only this time I aim to kill him twice. Just to make sure he don't come back to life again." He laughed at his own crude humor and his men laughed along with him, mostly because they knew that their life depended on it.

Then Jens motioned to the two men who rode behind me. He wanted them to circle around and come up into the valley below the ridge from the other side. Just like he'd done the last time he shot Patrick. He was making a mistake. He was violating his policy of not doing the same thing twice.

Riley noticed the error and grinned, knowing that the two riders would soon be dead. Two down. The three that were left were in front of him, which was a tactical advantage. The only worry being that one of them was Jens, who was unpredictable.

They waited, to give the two riders time to circle around. While waiting, Jens approached Riley. He must have figured that Riley had outlived his usefulness. He drew his gun and aimed it at Riley's head. Knowing Jens reputation, Riley didn't hesitate. He jerked his gun from under his shirt and fired it at Jens. At the instant he fired it he felt a massive blow. There was nothing but black after that.

# CHAPTER FIFTY

*ROWDY HEARD THE GUNFIRE* and panicked. It wasn't part of the plan. The first shots fired were supposed to be his and Shawn's and Patrick's, as a result of their ambush. Something had gone wrong. He left his hiding place behind a rock and circled back around to where Shawn had been posted. When he met up with him, Shawn was in the same uncertain state of confusion as Rowdy.

Together they decided to abandon the plan and round up the crew and run. They headed for Patrick's place of concealment, but when they arrived, he was gone.

"What do we do now?" Rowdy asked.

"There's no question where the boy went," Shawn answered. "The question is, do we really want to follow him."

"We'd probably be walking into an ambush," Rowdy said, understanding Shawn's drift.

"Yep."

"But do we have a choice?" Rowdy reasoned.

"Nope."

Patrick had gone to retrieve Josefina of course. She was the bait. At the sound of the first shot fired he knew there was something wrong and he dashed to her aid. Shawn and Rowdy were about to follow in his tracks, making them all bait.

They had only taken a few steps when Rowdy heard a noise behind them. He held a hand out to Shawn, indicating he should stop. They turned around just in time. There were two of Jens' men ten paces away, and they were holding guns.

Without hesitation Rowdy dove in one direction and Shawn in the other. They drew their weapons as they dove. Their quick reactions saved their lives, the bullets of Jens' men barely missing them.

Rowdy rolled twice before springing up on one knee and firing at the last place he had seen his attackers. They had moved a little and he adjusted his aim and fired several more shots. Shawn's gun roared to life in the same instant as Rowdy's. Their bullets found their marks and Jens' two men fell to the ground. They weren't dead, yet, and were groaning and writhing in pain. Shawn and Rowdy approached them warily, guns trained on them in case they were playing possum. When they got closer they saw enough blood and other signs to know that they'd been hit hard enough to keep them from causing any harm.

The one closest to Rowdy, a small red headed man, was shot low in the gut. The other one, a lanky dark haired young man had been shot high up on the right side of his chest. He was already wheezing and frothing blood at the mouth.

Rowdy was about to order the men to throw their guns toward him but he was preempted by Patrick's voice.

"What the hell!" Patrick hollered.

Shawn turned toward Patrick but Rowdy kept his eyes trained on Jens' men. He told them to throw their guns. The gut shot man did as he was told, but the young dark haired one was hurt too badly to move. His gun was out of his grip, lying on the ground nearby. Rowdy walked over and picked it up, then retrieved the gun that the red head had thrown.

Shawn covered Rowdy while he retrieved the wounded men's guns. He glanced toward Patrick and saw that he was not alone, he had hold of Josefina's arm with one hand, and Wind's lead rope with the other. Josefina appeared just a bit angry. Patrick was dragging her by the wrist, and not having an easy time doing it.

"What happened?" Patrick asked. "What the hell is all the shooting?"

"We don't know what the first shots were all about," Shawn told him. "But these two on the ground tried to ambush us and we shot em."

"Holy shit," Patrick said. "What went wrong?"

"We don't know," Shawn answered. He looked at Josefina. "You OK?" he asked her.

"Jes, senor. But not my arm where Patrick is hurting me," she informed them.

"Oh, sorry," Patrick said, releasing her arm. She rubbed it, looking at him with hurt in her eyes. Wind snorted, like he might be agreeing with Josefina's indignation. Patrick eyed him curiously. He turned back to Josefina.

"I was just scared that you'd get hurt, that's all," he explained to her. Her look lost a few daggers, but she wasn't smiling.

"Anyone seen Riley?" Shawn asked.

Nobody had. They debated what to do. They heard no more shooting, but that could be a bad sign or a good one, depending on why.

"Let's circle back around to the road and see if we can find Riley," Shawn suggested.

"What about these two?" Rowdy asked, pointing at the two outlaws.

"We could finish them off and then we wouldn't have to worry about them any more," Shawn said. The others looked at him with shock. "Or maybe not," he said.

"Patrick, you go get Josefina's horse and bring it back here. We don't want anyone running off with it. Then you stay here with Josefina and watch these two," Rowdy said. "We'll look for Riley. Wait here for us to return. Anything goes wrong fire a shot. We'll come runnin."

"I think I can handle that," Patrick said. He rode off on Wind to get Josefina's horse and was back in a couple of minutes.

# CHAPTER FIFTY ONE

*I KEPT A CLOSE EYE ON THE TWO OUTLAWS,* but not because I was worried about them doing anything harmful. I was more worried about Josefina's piercing eyes. The looks she'd been giving me were not particularly wholesome. Besides, the two men were shot bad, and I figured they were good as dead. That worried me too because once they were dead I would have no excuse to ignore Josefina's mean looks.

"Ju no haf to looking at thos mens," she said to me. I wondered again if she was able to read my mind. It was a frightening thought. "They will not do some thing," she explained. "They hurt bad."

"You never know," I answered. "They could be playing possum." My cowardly excuse for not facing her.

"And ju maybe are a ballena what can fly like a bird," she said. I'd never heard the word ballena before.

"I'm a what?" I asked.

"A very large fish, a wall," she said.

"You mean a whale?"

"Jes. One that fly."

It finally dawned on me what she was trying to say and I laughed so hard I got tears. She got caught up in my laughter and I could tell she was resisting it, but she wasn't able to stop herself from laughing with me. We both laughed and hung on to each other until I kissed her. Then things changed. There was no more laughing. We hugged each other tightly, expressing the panic we had shared moments ago, when we both wondered if she was in dire straits.

When we were done hugging I pushed back from her so that I could see her face, and look into her eyes. I saw anger in her eyes and a second later she hit me in the chest.

"What was that for?" I asked, insulted and hurt. It didn't physically hurt, but my feelings were bruised.

"Ju pull me around like I am ju caballo. And mira, ju hurt my arm." She held out her arm and I could see red welts above her wrist where I had roughly pulled her, I thought to safety at the time.

"I'm sorry," I told her sheepishly. "I wasn't trying to treat you like a horse. I don't think of you as a horse either. I was scared and I thought you were in danger. I panicked. I can't bear the thought of losing you."

"Why ju no like to lose me?" she asked me. She asked it without anger or resentment and I thought the change in her attitude was rather sudden. It made me wonder. But it didn't make me wonder enough, because if it had I would have known that she was never really angry to begin with, and that her act was all part of a plan. I still had a lot to learn about women I guess.

"Because I love you, Josefina. More than life," I told her. She smiled in response to that. And it was such a beautiful smile that I lost what little senses I had to start with. In other words, if I had any sense at all I would have realized that I had arrived at the very point that she had been leading me to all along, saying the exact words she expected to hear. Wind, who was tethered to a nearby tree must have understood what happened though, because he let out a quick whinny, that might have sounded like a laugh.

But, to be honest, even if I had a lick of sense at the time, I might have acted the same way and said the same things. They were honest words, and, if I'd had the courage along with my senses, I would have said them. Either way, Josefina was happy, and that was all that mattered.

"So what should we do with them?" I wondered out loud, pointing to the dying men. Remorse, pity, sympathy, regret, or any such feeling was as remote from my world as an emotion can get, and I wondered if I was becoming a little bit like Riley.

"Simple," she said. "Ju can kill now, or ju can do no thing and they die later. I no care." She seemed to have as little feeling on the matter as I did.

"Then I would rather do nothing," I said. Maybe I wasn't much like Riley after all. Or maybe I just did not have the same courage he had.

"Ju want them for suffer," she stated, nodding her approval. It wasn't really why I didn't want to kill them now, but since she seemed happy with the reason I let her believe it was true. In truth I didn't have the guts to finish them off. But I had considered it briefly, which meant I was changing. A little.

I put my gun down and ignored the wounded men. Josefina and I pondered our next move. Should we stay here as Rowdy suggested, or go looking for him and Pa. They'd been gone longer than I expected and I worried that they could have met trouble. We were debating the matter when we heard a rustle of leaves. I raised my gun again, ready for action. It was Pa and Rowdy.

"Josefina, we need your help here," Pa said. He and Rowdy were dragging Riley between them, one of his arms over each of their shoulders. He looked bad. Pa looked mortified by Riley's condition. Josefina jumped into action.

"We need a good place for him to lay," Pa said. I found a patch of grass and piled some loose leaves up on it. They laid him down gently on the pile of leaves. Riley moaned. Not that long ago I hated the man, now I couldn't stand to see him suffering.

"Do something, Josefina," I called to her desperately. I tried to avoid looking at his wound, not willing to face it if it was mortal. Backing down again, I realized. Then I realized how dangerous my gutless condition was. Someone could die while I was busy running away from my discomfort of their predicament. Riley could die. No more, I told myself. No more running. No more backing down. Sure, I was still scared. Possibly I was still terrified, but I wouldn't let my terror control me any longer. I looked at his wound, which was clearly visible now that Josefina had already removed the clothing from around it.

He was hit high on the right side of his chest. Possibly only damaging the shoulder. It could have been much worse and I was relieved at that concession. I was also relieved that my decision to face the horrible truth of his condition didn't immediately cause me irreversible mental damage. I was more or less the same person I had been a few moments ago. Except that now I was wondering why I had always been such a coward.

Josefina tended Riley's wound as best she could given the conditions and lack of medical supplies. She cleaned it with some fresh water, then applied a fresh bandage that she somehow magically withdrew from within her dress. I was going to have to explore that storage area someday. But not today. Today, right now, she asked me to go gather some yucca plants.

"Some what?" I asked.

"Never mind," she said. "Ju are no of use. Here, hold this cloth on him. Push hard." She ran off, I supposed to gather the plant she needed. I pushed on the bandage as I was instructed and looked into Riley's eyes. I expected to see a vision of desperation. The look of a man who is at deaths door, and I readied myself for it despite my own anguish. But he was smiling at me, which confused me. And his eyes were mischievous, which encouraged me.

"That son of a bitch thought he had me," Riley said to me. I was astounded. And very relieved. "All of you were right," he continued.

"He is one of the more evil creatures roaming this earth. If you hadn't warned me of that, I would be dead right now."

"What happened?" I asked him. Pa and Rowdy leaned in toward him, wanting to know the story as much as I did. Riley coughed and the pain caused by the effort of it showed plainly on his face. His eyes shut tightly, forcing tears out of their corners. We waited for him to regain his speech. Before he could, Josefina had returned, carrying a plant that I recognized but had never known it's name. Not it's real name anyway. In my mind it came under the general category of cactus. I had never dreamt it was medicinal.

"Go away," she ordered. I obeyed. I was learning.

Josefina did something things with the plant that I will not even attempt to describe, other than to say that the result of it was applied to Riley's wound. Then she stood back and looked at him, worry in her eyes. I didn't like seeing the worry in her eyes. She was the one who knew better than the rest of us, and if she was worried, then we should be too. But about what?

"What's wrong?" I asked her.

"Nothing," she answered. But she still looked worried. "Not jet," she clarified. "We see later if he get the feber."

"I got a bullet in him," Riley managed to gasp. Then he closed his eyes, exhausted. I jerked my head to look at him. Could he possibly be talking about Jens? Pa and Rowdy perked up as well.

"You mean Jens?" Pa asked.

"Yes," Riley whispered. Then he passed out.

# CHAPTER FIFTY TWO

*"I CAN'T BELIEVE IT," PA SAID,* stunned. We were all stunned. Could it be? Jens was shot? Riley got him? Was he dead?

"You think he killed him?" I asked.

"I hope so," Pa said. "But if he didn't, that means he's wounded. And if he's wounded and on the run, we have to move quick. We need to get him now, before he can make even the slightest recovery."

"How do we do that?" I asked him. He thought for a minute before answering me. I could see that he was trying to come up with a plan. He glanced at Josefina, then frowned. Then he glanced at Riley and frowned a little deeper. The he looked at the two wounded men on the ground, but he didn't frown. He walked up close to them and pulled his gun out of it's holster. He aimed it at one of them.

"I'm sorry," I heard pa say to him. "But you brought this on yourself when you made the choice to join up with the likes of Jens." Then without hesitation he pulled the trigger and shot the man in the heart. The man was instantly still. Instantly dead.

My emotions leapt into my throat. My heart was racing and I felt a wave of nausea. Memories of when Cal had been shot flooded my vision, gun-smoke assaulted my nose and burned my eyes. I walked in slow circles, looking for a path of reason, into which to take my mind. Before finding one, I heard another gunshot. I stopped circling and looked over at the other wounded man, who was now as dead as his friend. Then pa spoke.

"Now we have one less problem to worry about," he said. But it barely registered with me.

"You just murdered two men," I told him. I was in shock. I had seen several killings recently, and they were alarming. But somehow it felt different this time. It was harder for me to keep a distance between me and the killing when it was my own pa doing the shooting.

"Had no choice, son," he said. "There was nothing we could do for them. Watching them die would not only waste our time, but it would have been cruel to them." I couldn't move and pa had to put his arm around me as he guided me towards our horses. Rowdy and Josefina struggled with helping Riley walk back to our camp.

While we walked, pa was giving us instructions. My mind still felt a little dreamy, but I was starting to pull out of my shock. I listened to pa for direction.

"Josefina, you stay here with Riley," he said. "Fix him up the best you can. And don't let him die." Then he turned to me and said, "And you are staying with her in case any of Jens men come back." I nodded. Pa and Riley mounted their horses and rode off at a lope.

"What can I do to help?" I asked Josefina.

"Get water," she said. "And make a fire for to boil it." I did as I was told and a within thirty minutes we had boiling water.

"Where do you want the water?" I asked her.

"Put here, next to me," she instructed. She used the water to bathe Riley's wounds. He moaned a little, and it looked like he was not fully conscious. If he were, I would have loved to hear the story of what happened between him and Jens. Mostly so I could get a clear idea of how badly Jens was shot. Clearly I was hoping it was a mortal wound.

Josefina used some more of the boiled water to mix with the yucca plant. Then she applied the concoction to Riley's wound, wrapping a bandage over it.

"Will he be able to talk soon?" I asked Josefina.

"No se," she said. "Maybe jes, maybe not ever." She shrugged. I envied her ability to deal with conditions like this without panic. I wondered if it had to do with her past. Maybe she'd grown up around violence. Or maybe it was just a natural part of who she was.

When she was finished cleaning Riley's wound and bandaging it, I made her a cup of coffee and we sat down to relax. She looked fatigued. She looked worried. She looked like the most beautiful thing I had ever seen. I stared at her, trying to come up with the reason she took a liking to me.

"What?" she asked.

"What do you mean?"

"Why Ju look at me with that eyes?"

"Oh, sorry. I was just wondering how come someone as pretty as you wants to have anything to do with me."

"Ju have no thing wrong with Ju, Patrick. Ju are bery good mans. Why Ju no think it is true?" It was a good question, but it might take me quite a lot of time to come up with an acceptable answer. The first thing that jumped into my mind however, was the word Milksop McGee. How could I explain that to her?

"You may have a unique opinion of me," I told her.

"No, Patrick. Senor Rowdy tell me same thing. He like you."

"Ok," I conceded. "You and Rowdy have a unique opinion of me."

"And senor, Cal," she responded. "Ju think he no love Ju? And Antonio? And thos cowboys Ju help to bring the cows?" I guess I'd never thought about it that way, and the realization that she was right almost bowled me over. It was the first time in my life that I felt accepted. At least by more people than just pa and Josefina. I was almost ashamed that the acceptance by so many had gone unnoticed by me. I wondered how it had happened. Not my lack of noticing, but my general acceptance by people. Had I changed that much since leaving home?

I didn't ponder the question for long, though. Wind became restless, and was pawing the ground, wide eyed. When he started snorting I was sure that there was something dangerous nearby. I stood, drawing my gun, alert for danger. I circled around the fire, trying to get a clear view into the brush. I heard a muted rustling and stood still, trying to make out what it was. But there was no further sound. I stayed still for several more minutes, listening, watching. Nothing.

I walked to Wind, who was still uneasy. I followed his gaze, but still couldn't see what it was that had him upset. I glanced at Josefina's horse, but he seemed not to be worried. He only looked at Wind, probably wondering the same thing I was. What was he so uneasy about?

"Patrick," I heard Josefina whisper. I looked at her and she was nodding toward a small mound of dirt about forty yards from our camp. Then she made a gesture with her finger, indicating I should circle around and come up behind it.

I did what she suggested, moving silently and slowly. When I got behind the small hill I saw a man. I moved back defensively when I first spotted him, but he'd had his hands in the air so I approached him again, still carefully. His guns were already on the ground, making me wonder what he was up to. He didn't wait for me to ask.

"Don't shoot me," he said. "I'm quitting Jens."

"Move away from the guns," I ordered him. He did as he was told, and when I thought he was far enough away from them, I retrieved them. I stared at him, still suspicious. I didn't know how far to trust him. He didn't have a gun any more, so I didn't feel immediately threatened. But once he was in our camp he would have to be watched closely, in case he was a spy. Or something worse, like a provider of false information, intended to lead us into a trap.

"What do you want?" I asked him.

"I don't want to be part of Jens' gang any more. Maybe I should have quit a long time ago, but it's too late to worry about that now. I won't live long now, unless Jens is dead. So my best chance to leave him, and still live, is to team up with somebody who is aiming to kill him. I figure that's you and your group. You trapped us here, and you almost got him. I decided then that it was a good time for me to make my try at leaving." He sounded convincing, but I wasn't about to buy into his story yet.

I walked him into camp at gunpoint and told Josefina to feed him and give him some coffee, but I never holstered my gun. I kept it aimed at him while he ate.

"What's your name?" I asked him.

"Jason," he said. "Jason Everett."

"How long you been riding with Jens?" I asked him. I wanted to know how dedicated he was to Jens' group.

"Too long," he said. Not what I wanted to know.

"Exactly?" I asked.

"Couple of months," he said. If it was true, it made him a little less of a threat. It meant that he'd come to his senses quickly, and was possibly well intentioned, no matter how he'd ended up with Jens' gang. But how would I know if he was lying? Josefina.

"You know this man?" I asked her.

"No," she said. Her answer indicated that he had not been in Wichita while Josefina was there. If he was, Josefina would have seen him.

So it was not likely that he was lying, but there was no guarantee of that. He could have been with Jens, but not been around Wichita, or the saloon that Josefina worked in.

"Why did you join with him?" I asked.

"Not for any reason that will make you think I'm innocent."

# CHAPTER FIFTY THREE

"*WHERE IS YOUR HORSE?*" I asked Jason.

"I tied him to a tree yonder," he said, nodding his head in the direction of the horse. "I wanted to come into your camp without spooking you. Figured I'd have less chance of being shot that way." He had a point. Charging into camp would have got him shot. On the other hand, he could have rode up close and then hollered, 'Hello the camp', which was how people normally approached an unknown camp. Still, I figured, we were all under tense conditions.

"Josefina, go get his horse." She left to retrieve Jason's mount while I kept my gun trained on him. He stayed still, which was a smart thing to do, seeing as I was a novice to situations like this, which made me nervous. Which made me more dangerous to Jason.

Josefina returned with his horse, which verified that he was being truthful about one thing at least. She tied the horse up alongside Wind and Josefina's horse, Cabo. Then she went to Riley, tending to his wounds.

"Who is that?" Jason asked.

"The man who shot Jens," I told him. Then I watched his eyes for his reaction to the news, hoping it might give me a clue to his true intentions. He smiled.

"If he got a bullet into Jens," he said, "he's one hell of a man. Even if he had to take a bullet doing it, no one else has been able to." I still couldn't get a take on the man. He seemed sincere enough, but I could hardly afford to trust anyone who came from Jens' camp. Then he noticed his two dead comrades.

"You shoot those two?" he asked me.

"No," I said.

"Then how'd they die?"

"My pa and another man shot them," I answered. He didn't have any response to that.

"Friends of yours?" I asked him.

"Not really. I knew them, but only recently. They were hard cases," he said.

"Like you?"

"Maybe," he said.

"Like how?" He hesitated after my question. "Well?"

"Well, whatever I tell you isn't going to help my cause," he said. I snorted a laugh.

"Mister, right now you have no cause," I informed him. "The only reason I haven't shot you already is that I'm new to this game, and I'm a bit murder shy." I snorted another laugh to emphasize my anxiety. "So talk, before I lose my nerve and shoot you out of self preservation." I think there was more menace in my voice than I had intended, or known I was capable of. He looked a little worried by my threat, which was something I was not used to seeing.

"Ok," he said. "I ain't no saint, alright? I've been an outlaw for much longer than a couple of months. It's a long story, but I never intended to ride outside the law, it just happened. I mean, I ran into hard times, and when I was faced with the real possibility of starvation, I became desperate. The first opportunity that came along, I took it. It weren't legal though. I had to rustle cows. I hated it, but it fed me. I lived, and there weren't many other options coming my way. So I crossed the line and rode with the bad guys. That was several years ago. Then I was approached by one of Jens' men, who sung his praises. He told me how rich I could be if I joined up with his gang. I didn't know a thing about Jens, but I knew I needed more money, so I signed on.

"Didn't take me too long to figure out what kind of man Jens was. But by that time I wasn't able to walk away without fear of being hunted down and killed. Then you guys came along." I considered what he told me for while. It boiled down to the fact that he didn't mind bending the law when it helped him survive, but when it became a matter of outright murder, nothing to do with staying alive, he didn't cotton to it. I could see his reasoning.

"When did you decide that you'd crossed the line?" I asked him. "From just plain criminality to something else?" He snorted a laugh and nodded in acceptance of my distinction.

"You're right. I think it took an extreme example of life outside the law to convince me that I was way too far down the wrong path. But if any person in the world can provide that example, it's Jens. That man is the epitome of evil." His choice of words was what ultimately convinced me that he may be telling me the truth about his situation. Not many people, especially criminals, have the type of vocabulary that Jason was using. Words like 'epitome' were seldom heard in the west. Hell they were seldom heard anywhere in America. But I had an education, so I could perceive his use of words.

"Where did you go to school," I asked him. He seemed surprised by the question.

"I think I'm done answering you're questions," he said. I recognized his reluctance. Like Bill Hardy said, I might not want to pry, if it meant I could bring trouble on myself. Jason was trying to protect me from something. But what?

"What's your real name?" I asked him. He broke eye contact with me and I knew I'd lost him. We both remained silent for a while. I'm sure he was thinking completely different thoughts than I was thinking, because I raised by gun back up, aiming it at his heart.

"Wrong answer," I said, as I pulled back the hammer of my Colt 44.

"Whoa," he said instantly. I recognized that word. It meant stop. If only Wind had known, I thought. I lowered my gun, but the meaning in my stare was clear.

"Ok, you're right," he admitted. "Keep your gun down. I'll tell you."

# CHAPTER FIFTY FOUR

"*MY NAME IS NOT JASON EVERETT,*" Jason Everett said. Of course that statement did nothing to increase my confidence in the man. Factually, it only increased my suspicions.

"Really?" I asked him. "So who are you really? Doc Holiday?" I think I hit a nerve. He cringed.

"I am a U.S. Marshal." OK, that got my attention.

"Bullshit."

"Look in my saddlebags."

I walked to his horse and looked inside his saddle bags. There were the usual items, and then there was a badge. I looked at it carefully. The name on it was Lawrence K. Kelly. U.S. Marshal. It was evidence but I wasn't fully convinced. Maybe he stole it from a deputy, or had a fake one made for him. I had never seen a Marshal's badge before, so how was I to know?

"So what was that story you just told me, about crossing the line, and being driven across it by dire conditions?" I demanded.

"My cover story," he said. "To get me into the gang. There is a real Jason Everett, but we have him locked up. I used his history, hoping it would be convincing, and in case someone recognized his name. If they did, it would corroborate my tale."

"What's your mission?"

"Get Jens behind bars, of course," he told me.

"What took you so long. Why didn't you grab him two months ago, and save a bunch of lives?" He looked away from me again, and I believed that I had shamed him with my question.

"That was another little lie I told you," he said, looking up at me again. "I only just got into the gang yesterday."

"So why are you quitting so soon?" Again he had a sheepish look.

"I saw someone looking in my saddle bags this morning, just before we left to come here," he explained. "I think Jens planned on shooting me out here. When I heard shots, and people were scattering, I took the opportunity to get away from them." Neither of us spoke for a while. I needed time to consider everything he told me. I think I believed him, mostly due to his educated way of speaking. And there was really no reason for him to carry a badge unless it was for real.

I asked Josefina to get us some coffee, then I sat down. I kept my gun handy and made it clear to Lawrence that he should not move. He was happy to sit still and drink his coffee. Riley moaned again, and Josefina went to him.

"There is a kit in my saddle bags," Kelly said. "It has some medicine in it that will help keep out the infection. Go ahead and use it." I nodded to Josefina who retrieved the kit from his bags.

"Thank Ju, senor," she told him. He nodded.

We sat silent again. My thoughts turned to pa and Rowdy. They were riding into danger, and I wished I was with them. I didn't wish for the danger, I just hated sitting here helplessly, and not knowing if they were OK.

# CHAPTER FIFTY FIVE

*WHEN ROWDY AND SHAWN HAD RIDDEN* out of camp they had no trouble finding a trail of blood to follow. According to Riley it would have to be Jens' blood. There were plenty of other horse tracks alongside Jens', he was not alone. Rowdy suggested that they make a plan, rather than ride blindly into a nest of bad guys. It was a good idea to have a smart plan, but not so easy to think one up.

Initially they agreed to slow up, be more cautious, and try to keep a clear view of the trail ahead of them. That would lessen the chances of them riding into an ambush.

"You have any idea where they might be headed?" Shawn asked Rowdy. Rowdy shrugged, but was considering the question.

"Couple of possibilities I can think of," he said. "But it's nothing I can be certain of."

"Let's hear it."

"Maybe they are taking a roundabout way back to town. Jens needs doctoring kind of badly."

"Is there a doctor in the town?" Shawn asked.

"Not really. Couple of women are handy with minor stuff." Shawn nodded. Rowdy was right, nothing to be too sure of.

"Where's the nearest doctor?" he asked. Rowdy had to think about that a minute.

"If he needs help fast, then he's looking for a doctor he can get to the quickest, not necessarily the closest one. And he'll need a damn good doctor too. Not a small town drunk one. That means he'd be going to Kansas City," he said.

"How do you figure that?"

"He can take the train." Shawn understood his reasoning.

"So we need to beat him to the train."

"Yep. He's not trying to catch it in town, either. That's too far to ride. He's going straight for the tracks."

"How do we get on that train first?" Shawn asked.

"We ride like hell. We go southwest. The train will be coming from that direction, heading to Wichita and then on to Kansas City. If we get on it a little further south, we can be on it when Jens stops it. But we'd have a few more miles to ride than he does," Rowdy explained.

"Let's go then," Shawn said.

They spurred their mounts and headed southwest. They couldn't run the horses flat out, because it was too far, they wouldn't make it. They had to lope some, then slow down to let the horses catch their wind again. After a couple of hours of that Shawn said, "I wish we had Wind." Rowdy agreed.

They rode as hard as they dared, saving the horses, and after a few hours they spotted the train tracks. They stopped at the edge of the rail bed and looked up and down the tracks.

"Damn it," Rowdy swore. Shawn looked in the direction of Rowdy's stare. He saw what Rowdy saw, a plume of smoke rising in the air. From the smokestack of a train. A train that was traveling away from them. They had missed it.

"What now?" Shawn asked.

"Nothing we can do now," Rowdy answered. "Our horses are too played out to catch up with the train."

They walked their horses along the tracks, in the direction of the train. They topped a small hill, overlooking the valley where the train traveled. They watched it hopelessly as it stopped, and Jens' gang boarded it. Then it moved on again.

It was late in the day now, and the two men made camp for the night alongside the tracks. In the morning they, and their horses, were a little rested, if sore from the hard ride the day before. They started for the camp where they had left Riley, Josefina and Patrick. They tried not to think about their disappointed faces when they broke the bad news to them.

## CHAPTER FIFTY SIX

*I GREW TIRED OF WATCHING KELLY AFTER* about five hours of staring at him and pointing my gun in his direction. About two hours ago I'd asked Josefina to spell me, but she refused.

"Ju haf no reason for watch the mans," she'd said. "He es a Marshal." At least someone was convinced. I wished it were me, then I could get some rest.

"You're tired," Kelly told me. As if I didn't already know it. I didn't respond to him.

"What if they come back?" he asked me.

"Who?"

"Jens' and his boys." Again, I didn't answer him.

"You aim to take them all on, alone?" Good question. I'd been wondering the same thing for several hours. But no solution had come to me.

"What's the difference?" I asked him

"The difference is that if I had a gun, it would double our defenses," he said as if it was too obvious.

"Or take away all of mine," I countered.

"Your funeral," he said. He was right. But it was his as well if Jens' gang returned.

"Look," he said. "You could still cover me with your gun, even if I had one too. But at least if we were attacked, we would be on the same side." It made sense. All except the part where I would have to sleep very soon. Then who would watch him? Not Josefina.

Nature determined all of our fates when it put me to sleep. Several hours later, when I woke up, I was looking at the business end of a Colt 44. My Colt 44. I would have been embarrassed if I wasn't so frightened.

"How's it feel?" Kelly asked me. I didn't answer. What was the point.

"You're lucky," he said.

"How do you figure?"

"I really am a Deputy." He flipped the handle of the gun so that the handle was being offered to me, and the barrel was pointing back at him. He did it real fast, like he knew how to handle a handgun. I took it.

"Ok," I said, "Now we are back where we started. I have a gun, and you don't." He laughed.

"You sound mighty sure of that, for someone who's been asleep for so long." He drew a pistol from behind his back so quick that if he was aiming to shoot me I would have been dead before I saw it. Then he laughed.

"Like I said, you're lucky." He lowered his gun, and I took a breath. "I really am a Deputy, and we really do need to make a plan, in case Jens' gang really does return." He had a point I guess. But it was pointless at the same time.

"If his gang comes back we are all dead," I told him. "Even with our two guns it would be fatal. The best we could hope for would be prolonging our deaths long enough to cause a few of theirs."

"Better than the alternative," he said.

"What's the alternative?"

"We die without killing any of them."

"Okay," I said. "You've convinced me. Of what, I don't know for sure. But it's either that you are really a dedicated Deputy, or you are completely crazy." He laughed. I laughed. Josefina laughed. Then we stopped laughing. We heard horses coming.

# CHAPTER FIFTY SEVEN

*"HELLO THE CAMP," I HEARD PA HOLLER.* My relief was unimaginable, until I saw the look on his face. It had bad news written all over it. But at least he was alive, and that was what I'd been most worried about. Rowdy was unharmed as well, so I knew that they hadn't met with serious trouble.

Kelly and I took care of the horses for them while Josefina took care of Pa and Rowdy. The horses looked haggard, and their riders looked worse. They were alive,but it was plain that the ride had been a hard one. I noticed them looking squint-eyed at Kelly too, but I knew the explanation would have to wait a few minutes. They must have trusted the fact that I was comfortable with the man, and left it alone for the time being.

They asked about Riley and went to look him over. Then they drank some coffee and got some food in them.

After the horses were settled, and Pa and Rowdy had finished eating, I introduced Kelly.

"This is Lawrence K. Kelly," I told them. "He's a Deputy Marshal. He goes by Kelly." Kelly shook hands with Rowdy and Pa. They looked at him for a moment, as if trying to guess his story, but didn't speak to him. They had other business to talk about first.

"It's bad news I'm afraid," Pa said to us. "Jens got away on a train. Probably headed for Kansas City to get help from a decent doctor."

"So he was really shot then?" I asked.

"Yes. We seen the blood trail. And when he boarded the train he needed plenty of help from his men." There was silence after that. Each person weighing in their minds the consequences of the news. Kelly spoke first.

"It's a shame that he still walks the earth, that's for sure," he said. "But at least we know he won't be doing much killing for a while."

"True enough," pa said.

"But that's only a temporary state of affairs," Rowdy added. "Soon as he's well, he'll start killin again. He don't know nothin else."

"True enough," Kelly said. They sat silent again for a few minutes. Then it was Pa who spoke.

168

"What's your play in this?" he asked Kelly.

Kelly related the same story he had told me and Josefina, only this time he didn't bother with all the lies he told us when he first showed up. He got right to the meat of it.

"So do you aim to arrest him?" pa asked. Kelly shrugged. More silence. Then Rowdy piped up.

"I won't let you stop me from killing him, if that's what you're thinking," he stated.

"I hear you," Kelly replied. "But I'm bound by an oath to obey the law." Rowdy narrowed his eyes at him for a second.

"You are also bound by your honor as a human being to do the decent thing," he said. Kelly nodded.

"A lot of people have a lot of differing concepts of exactly what the right thing is," Kelly countered.

"You really want to get into that debate?" Pa asked.

"No," Kelly admitted. "I see the need for eliminating the man. But I can't be the one to do it, as a lawman. And I can't stand by and watch without trying to prevent it. No matter how much I agree with your assessment of the morality of killing him."

"Your just a man," Rowdy pointed out.

"I never claimed otherwise."

"So all kinds of things happen to men. Even deputies. For instance their horses step on a stone and get a bruised hoof, causing them to get held up on the trail." He paused here, waiting to see if his meaning was getting across. "Or maybe you eat something that poisons you, and you have to stay behind. Happens to all of us sometimes." He paused again and I could tell that Kelly was getting his point.

"Sure," Kelly said. "I'm only human after all. Any human tragedy could befall me, at any time." He smiled.

"Even at the most inopportune time," pa added. "It's happened to me before."

"I see," Kelly said, nodding his understanding. "And by 'inopportune' I assume you mean at the precise moment someone might be killing Jens."

"I see that you are a very smart man," Pa said.

# CHAPTER FIFTY EIGHT

*WE SPENT THE REST OF THE DAY* making our plans to rid the world of Jens. It was the second time I had to participate in that discussion, and there was still a foul taste in my mouth from the failure of the first plan. However, I did admit to myself that we had come damn close to succeeding. Riley got a shot at him, and almost killed him. Maybe it did kill him. If we were lucky, I thought, Jens would not survive the wound that Riley inflicted on him. On the other hand, Riley might not survive his own wound.

We made our plans on the assumption that both Riley and Jens would survive. Obviously if Jens didn't survive, no further plans were needed. But in case he did, we needed Riley. Either way our priority would be seeing to his recovery.

Kelly turned out to be a valuable source of information about Jens. A lot of what he told us we'd never heard before, and it was plain that the Marshals had been hard at work investigating the man for some time. His information provided better insight into Jens' routines and habitual methods of committing his crimes. We put the information to good use during the planning.

It was late by the time we completed our planning, and by then we were tired. There was a little more work to be done on the details, but it could wait til morning. We needed sleep.

Like always, Josefina arose early. She'd already seen to Riley, changing his bandages and feeding him some water and some broth. He'd had a rough night, we all heard him groaning, and a couple of times he yelled a little. I cringed when I heard how he was suffering, wishing I had some idea of how to help him. My feeling of helplessness hurt me badly. Josefina had tended to him as best she could whenever that happened, but there was only so much she could do.

She had coffee ready for us in the morning by the time we rolled out of our makins, and the beans and tortillas were heating on the fire. It wasn't fancy fare, but in our situation it smelled darn good.

After eating we got down to the business of finishing the details of our plan. Those details consisted of taking an inventory of our supplies, and then making a list of what we needed to add to it. Nothing fancy was on the list, just the important stuff, like bullets. We also added some more food supplies and bandages for Riley.

The first phase of our plan revolved almost entirely around Riley, so we really had to get him healed up. We had a little time though, Jens wasn't about to go anywhere until he healed up as well. We made use of the time by setting in supplies and reviewing the plan over and over, making little adjustments as the need came.

With Jens' gang gone off to Kansas City, we figured Wichita was a fairly safe town. But just in case any of them stayed behind, Pa and Kelly were designated to ride in and purchase our supplies. They were the least known faces there, but not entirely unknown. For that reason they would tie up the horses outside of town and Kelly would sneak in on foot to see who might be hanging around.

Rowdy was dispatched to Kansas City to gather intelligence on Jens and his condition, hoping against hope that it was dead. If it was not dead, we needed to know his situation there. The information was most vital to their plan.

Pa and Kelly were gone two days, while Josefina and I watched Riley and did the best we could for him. I won't lie and say we didn't take advantage of the privacy as well. I explored some new territory, and I did a little more growing up.

The two men returned to camp with just about all of the items we needed. They reported that a couple of Jens' men were still in town, but they hadn't made a fuss. We were stocked up now, and able to hang on in the camp while Riley got better.

It took him two weeks to heal enough that we were sure he was going to make it. It was rough two weeks for him, but he was a tough man, and at the end of it he was up and walking a little. A week later he was riding a horse.

PART SIX:  LIVE AND LEARN

IF AT FIRST YOU DON'T SUCCEED,
  DON'T DO IT OVER AGAIN.
    FIGURE OUT WHAT YOU DID WRONG,
    AND DO IT RIGHT NEXT TIME.

DOC BONNER

# CHAPTER FIFTY NINE

*WE WERE GLAD TO BE LEAVING CAMP.* The weeks of waiting, and with little to do, had made us restless. On the other hand we were relieved that Riley had recovered enough to ride a horse, making the wait worthwhile.

Our destination was Kansas City. We would meet up with Rowdy along the trail somewhere south of town, where he could brief us on Jens' condition. If he was dead, so much the better. If not, we had to hone our plan to include whatever details Rowdy could provide.

We took our time at first, going slow enough to make sure Riley could stand up to the ride. He made it through the first days ride, but at a cost. He fell unconscious as soon as we stopped for our first camp.

It took another day for Riley to come to his senses, but he was still in no shape for a long ride. It took him another day to be well enough to mount a horse. We rode more slowly this time, stopping more frequently to tend to him. He made it to the next camp without passing out, but he was close to it. We did what we could for him and turned in for the night. The next day he felt better and we started out again for Kansas City.

On the fourth day Riley did a little better. He was even a little humorous when we finally made camp.

"You all seem to have a keen liking for a death march," he said. Then he coughed and laughed at the same time. Tears came to his eyes, probably from the pain caused by the laughing. It made me admire the man. Then I recalled that day in his stable, when he gave me Wind, and I had hated him. What a far ways I had come since that day. Josefina seemed offended by his comment.

"Ju no even make yoke about death," she demanded. "Ju knows that mens get what they wish for, even if Ju say is yoke." She was so upset about it that it sobered us up and we stopped laughing. To be honest I didn't know what to make of what she'd said. But Riley took her seriously.

"Sorry, Josefina," he told her. "You're right. It's not good to joke about things like that."

173

Kelly was silent during the exchange, but he stared at Josefina like he was trying to recall where he had seen her before.

I was glad that Riley was looking better, and he could joke around some, whether proper or not. It was an uplifting improvement and our spirits were on high. We ate and debated the plan for ending Jens' evil reign, something we discussed obsessively these days.

Riley fell asleep first, and since I was on first watch I drank the last cup of coffee in the pot. I knew that Josefina would have another one going before waking up pa to spell me. Kelly had the night off. We alternated two nights on watch with one off to catch up on sleep.

Four hours into my watch I heard Josefina stirring. She stoked the fire and started a new pot of coffee. Pa heard her moving about and crawled out of his makins, pulling on his boots and yawning. He put on his gun belt and sat next to me.

"Any excitement so far?" he asked me. I knew he wasn't serious. He probably would have heard any trouble coming before I had, even in his sleep.

"Plenty," I told him. "But you missed it all. You slept right through it."

"Shame," he said. "Sleeping was really starting to bore me. I could have used a little excitement."

"Next time I'll wake you," I told him. Then I said goodnight and went to my bedroll, ready for some sleep. I watched Josefina take a cup of coffee to pa. Not that I cared about the cup, or the coffee, I just liked watching Josefina. Gave me something to dream about.

When I woke up, the first thing I saw was Josefina. I thought it was a good way to start the day, and I hoped it was an omen as well. Like always, she had the coffee hot and ready. I helped myself to a cup and then checked on Riley. He already had a fresh cup of coffee in his hands and he looked a little better today. Kelly was up as well, and was gabbing with Riley while drinking his coffee.

I walked over to pa. "Any excitement after I sacked out?" I asked him.

"Plenty," he said. "But you needed your rest, so I didn't wake you."

"Thanks," I said. "Appreciate it."

"No problem."

We repeated the routine for several more days. Riley gained strength day by day until one night he asked if he could take a watch. As much as we were relieved by his improvements, we didn't want to take the risk of him falling asleep. We explained as much to him and he took it well. I understood his desires. No man likes to be dependent on others if it can be helped. But he needed a little more time to heal up.

On the tenth day, Rowdy came into sight ahead of us on the trial.

# CHAPTER SIXTY

*"HOWDY, BOYS AND GIRL,"* Rowdy greeted us. He wore a big smile, happy to be back in the company of his friends.

"Hey there, Rowdy," Pa said in return. We stopped in the trail to make a brief reunion, saying hello, and how much we missed him, and he us, etc. But we couldn't hang around on the trail all day.

"There is a good camp site a few miles back up the trail," Rowdy informed us. "I already scouted it out. It looks safe enough." So we followed him back up the trail, and when we got to the site he had referred to, we climbed down from our horses and set up camp.

After we were settled into camp and seated around the fire, Rowdy began his debriefing.

"He's still alive," he informed us. "That's the bad news." We all nodded with acceptance, as if we'd expected it.

"How bad is he?" Riley asked. I figured he was wondering how good of shot he got into him.

"Worse than you, if that makes you feel any better. He won't be up and walkin around anytime soon."

"What's the layout there?" Pa asked, referring to Jens' defenses in Kansas City.

"That's the other bad news," Rowdy said. "He must be expecting trouble, because he is hemmed in tight. At least two of his men are by his side at all times. Sometimes more than two. And they aren't being lazy or gettin drunk. They are stayin alert. Like I said, they seem to expect an attack."

"Bad news maybe, but it's what we figured when we made out plans," Pa said. "Where is he holed up? What's the layout like?"

Rowdy explained the layout of the town itself, and the building that Jens was laid up in, using a stick to draw diagrams in the sand when needed. He covered all the details including the schedules and routines of his men. He had even inspected their remuda, assessing the value and condition of each of their horses. He inventoried their firearms and ammunition as best he could as well. He'd done a pretty thorough job of reconnaissance, and it proved to be vital in making a plan that had a chance of succeeding.

As important as Rowdy's intelligence was, Riley was also vital to our success. We needed every able body we could have. But he was not quite able bodied yet. So we bided our time, reviewing and perfecting our plan while doing all we could to help Riley heal up more completely. He needed to be more than just well. He needed to be fast with his gun and back to full strength.

Kelly was instrumental in coming up with a strategy. His experience in the matter of apprehending criminals was invaluable. Especially when it came to evaluating the specific abilities and advantages of each of us. He easily saw what part each of us would be best at playing.

Two weeks later we put Riley to the test. First we made him do some hard riding. He was tired afterward, but he held up.

Then, Pa sparred with him, like they had as lads growing up together. Riley held his own in the scrap, and even bloodied Pa's nose. Riley laughed at him when he saw the blood seeping from Pa's nose, and that made Pa bloody minded. He went after Riley in a rage and we had to restrain him. When he calmed down we explained to him that we were trying to get Riley healed up, not damage him further. Of course we all laughed about it when it was over.

Next, Kelly put Riley through some practice sessions with his gun, to see how well he could shoot under various circumstances. He shot well enough. After several other such trials we declared him fit. His reaction to the declaration was sobering.

"Thanks," he said. "I hope the commendation doesn't turn out to be my ticket to heaven."

"Don't worry about it," Pa told him. "I don't think you're headed there anyway."

"Thanks, Shawn," Riley told him. "I feel much better now."

# CHAPTER SIXTY ONE

*ON THE OUTSKIRTS OF KANSAS CITY* we stopped for camp. Our plans had been set long since, and we had gone over them a thousand times. Even so, we went over them again, one last time. By the time it had grown dark we were as ready as were ever going to be.

There would be no sleeping tonight. Our plan was to be carried out in the late hours of the night. According to Rowdy, Jens' protection system was the most relaxed during the late night hours. Most of his men were asleep, leaving a minimum guard detail. He kept one man stationed outside the door to his room, and another posted at the entrance to the hotel. Both of them had been observed napping during their watch, so they were vulnerable.

Rowdy never actually saw the inside of Jens' room, so if we succeeded in getting past the sentries and gained entrance to his room we were going to have to play it by ear. We had several options to choose from, according to what we encountered.

We would be arriving to town late, after midnight. Meantime, we checked our weapons and stocked extra ammunition. We filled our saddle bags and fed the horses plenty of grain, in case we needed to make a hard ride to make an escape. When midnight rolled around we were riding down the trail to Kansas City.

Josefina rode with us, but she was not going all the way into town. None of us were riding horseback into town as a matter of fact. We were going to walk for the last several hundred yards. It was important to our plan that we enter town as quietly and as unobserved as possible. Josefina's job was to watch the horses and have them ready when we returned for them.

We reached the point where we dismounted. I hated leaving Josefina alone, and had argued against the idea many times during our planning. I was always voted down, and now that the moment of leaving her had arrived, I had a terrible foreboding.

"I can't leave her here alone," I told pa.

"It's too late, Patrick," he said. "We have to move out, and we've already talked about it enough. I know it goes against your principle, but there's no other choice." I nodded sadly. I kissed Josefina and walked to Wind. He nudged me, like he was ready to keep riding. I hated leaving him behind almost as much as I hated leaving Josefina.

"Take care of my Josefina," I told him. "I'm counting on you." He put his head down, a dejected look on his face.

"Let's go," Pa said. As we started down the trail I looked back and saw Josefina watching us. Tears were running down her cheeks. I turned my eyes ahead of me on the trail, hating Jens even more for putting me in this situation.

# CHAPTER SIXTY TWO

*KANSAS CITY WAS QUIET.* The hour was late and the only sounds were coming from the saloon on Main Street. We could hear the muted sounds of a piano player banging out a listless tune. No doubt he was trying to entertain the die-hard poker players who were still gambling.

Rowdy had gone slightly ahead of the rest of us, verifying the position of the guards. When he returned, he confirmed that the guards were as expected, one in front of the hotel and one outside the door to Jens' room.

Now it was Riley's turn. He went into town, on his own, while we stayed back. He entered the hotel, approached the guard, and went into his drunken act. We had poured some whiskey on his clothes and he kept a large gulp of it in his mouth to give his breath the correct odor. He walked toward the guard with a stagger and a loud, unintelligible slur of words. As the guard rose out of his chair to fend off the drunken Riley, he was greeted by a sharp bowie knife to the heart. It was silent, and it was deadly. Riley held the man up while his last breath expired and then laid him gently back in his chair. He arranged his hat and his limbs to appear as if he was asleep.

The rest of us approached quietly after the guard was subdued. Riley and Pa went into the hotel by the main entrance while me and Rowdy went to the back of the hotel and entered through the back door. Pa and Riley kept an eye on the lobby while Kelly stayed out in the street, watching for accidental intruders, or more of Jens' gang.

The job of killing Jens had been left to me and Riley. We were the ones who had been shot by him directly, and it was voted early on in our plans that we should have the honors. The others were obliged to keep a watch for anyone who may interfere with us.

We approached the stairway to the second floor slowly and walked up the steps as quietly as possible. At the top of the stairs I peeked around the corner and glimpsed the guard outside the door to Jens' room. He was asleep. I motioned to Riley that the coast was clear. He moved fast and pistol whipped the guard before he even had a chance to wake up. There was nothing standing between us and Jens now.

———————

On the streets in front of the hotel all was quiet. Kelly had a clear view of the area and nobody was moving. Pa and Rowdy could see no one in the hotel lobby. As they had hoped, there would be no interference with their plans tonight.

# CHAPTER SIXTY THREE

*JOSEFINA WAS RESTLESS.* She was sure that something was wrong. She was not sure why she felt so sure about the fact, and she had no idea what it was that was so wrong. But that did nothing to reduce her resolve on the matter. Something was wrong.

She figured that the horses were the only thing of interest to bad men so she checked and double checked every horse in her care. She checked their ties. She checked their tack and their feed. She watched their temperament, looking for any signs that they were as worried as she was, but she saw no indications of trouble. The lack of evidence did not comfort her. On the contrary, it made her even more alert.

She knew from experience that a loose horse could be difficult, maybe impossible, to catch. But a tied horse was not much of a challenge to capture. Therefore she retied the horses, using a slip knot that her father had taught her. If the horses pulled hard against it, it would come undone. It was a trick that was normally used to break a horse of the habit of pulling back when it was tied up. But in this case Josefina used the slip tie to allow the horses to escape if they became frightened. And if a horse thief came into camp, she knew just how to make them frightened.

After seeing to the horses she built up the fire to make it bright. Then she slipped back into the bushes, away from the light cast by the flames. Hidden by the darkness, she waited. And watched.

# CHAPTER SIXTY FOUR

*RILEY AND I HAD A SECRET AGREEMENT.* He had agreed to allow me first crack at Jens. We didn't necessarily hide our agreement from the others so much as we thought that it was a personal thing, between just the two of us. We shared something unique. Something the others had not experienced. And as a result Riley understood my feelings about Jens. Therefore, he knew how deep my hatred for Jens was. And therefore, he granted me first rights to kill him. So after he disabled the guard at Jens' door he motioned to me to enter the room.

I braced myself for a second and then burst through the door, rolling instinctively to avoid a counter attack by Jens. There were no sounds of gunfire, and no other sounds either. I peered up over the edge of the bed trying to get Jens in my sights, but I saw nothing. I stood up and searched the bed. Nothing. I searched the room. Nothing. Jens was gone.

Riley entered the room, wondering why he hadn't heard gunfire.

"What are you waiting for?" he whispered.

"I'm waiting for Jens to show up," I told him in a loud voice. He looked around the room and soon understood what I meant.

# CHAPTER SIXTY FIVE

*JOSEFINA HOVERED IN THE BUSHES,* remaining still and silent for several minutes before hearing a faint rustle of leaves, like someone was walking on them. She listened more closely. The sounds she heard did not sound natural, not like any animal sounds that she was familiar with. It had to be human, but it was not like any human sounds she had heard before either. She remained silent, waiting, listening.

A figure came into the firelight. She wasn't sure at first what it was or who it was. It was a man, she could tell that much. He approached the fire, looking around the camp cautiously. When he got close to the fire she could make out Jens face. He was dragging one of his feet, with a limp, which explained the strange sounds he made.

A shiver when up her spine. The evil man was here. And she was alone. How could this have happened, she wondered. Por que Dios?

There was nothing she could do except remain where she was and not make a sound. If she was lucky Jens would not notice her. She watched him examine the ground, taking stock of the footprints. She knew that there were many boot prints left by the men who had gone into town on foot, and she prayed that Jens would be swayed by them and believe that he was outnumbered. But when he smiled she knew he had figured it out. He knew that the men had left the camp, gone into town. And he knew that she was still here. She shuddered.

# CHAPTER SIXTY SIX

*"WHAT THE HELL," RILEY SAID.*

"You tell me," I answered him. "Looks like Rowdy missed something."

"Not something," he said back, "more like someone. Like Jens." We were about to go find Rowdy and ask him about it, but he beat us to it, walking into the room. He took a quick look around and noticed something was missing.

"What the hell," he said.

"Exactly," me and Riley said at once.

"This isn't good," Rowdy added. It seemed like an inadequate statement if you asked me.

"No shit, Rowdy," I said. "What does it mean? Was he ever here? You said you never saw him."

"I didn't, but I'm sure he was here," he told us. "I saw food brought in and empty plates taken out. I saw the doc come and go with bloody bandages. He was here alright."

"Then how do you explain this?" I asked.

"I can't."

"Great." Possibilities began to appear in my mind. There were only two of them. Either he just happened to step out, to use the toilet or something. Or he knew we were coming. Unfortunately the second possibility seemed the most likely.

"He knew we were coming," I told Rowdy and Riley.

"How do you figure," Rowdy asked me.

"There was a guard outside his door," I informed them. "If he left the room to take a leak or something, the guard would have gone with him. That means the guard stayed outside his door to makes us think that Jens was still in the room."

"Makes sense," Rowdy agreed. Riley nodded his own agreement. Then Kelly walked into the room.

"What happened?" he asked.

185

"Nothing," I informed him. "Jens is gone. He knew we were coming."

"How?"

"I'm not sure. Maybe he had lookouts on the trail. Maybe he just felt it in his bones," I explained. "We already know he has some kind of way of knowing. Remember what Josefina said about him?"

"Yeah," Rowdy said, "She said he was not from this earth. And that he could tell what you were thinking."

"Right. So maybe that's what happened. Or maybe not," I said. "But either way, he out-foxed us. And I don't like it."

"So, if he knew we were coming, and he set his guard at his door to fool us, where did he go?" Riley asked.

Josefina! It struck me instantly. He was after the horses. That meant Josefina was in danger.

# CHAPTER SIXTY SEVEN

*"HELLO, PRETTY SENORITA,"* Jens said. "I know you can hear me. I can feel you. You're here, somewhere. Where are you hiding? Come out and say hi to your old friend, Jens."

Josefina shuddered again, harder this time. Evil was upon her. She prayed, silently. And she didn't move, not even to breathe. The monster had her in his sights, and she was terrified. She could not think of a way to escape him. If she moved, he would hear or see her. Even with his injured leg she was not confident she could outrun him. A normal man with an injured leg would not worry her, but Jens was not human. He'd proved that more than once. She could not run, but if she stayed where she was, he would eventually find her.

"All alone aren't you," Jens said into the darkness. "Not very manly of your friends to leave you here all alone is it?" He spoke quietly, almost a whisper, knowing that in the still of the night she would hear him.

The low voice was meant as a taunt as well, to instill even more fear into her. And it worked. She could hear her heart pounding so hard that she worried Jens would hear it as well. Her blood rushed through her so madly that it nearly took control of her body, compelling it to flee, and she found it nearly impossible to sit still. Through some kind of otherworldly sense, Jens worked his way slowly but directly toward her hiding spot. In only a minute more he would be able to see her, then all would be lost. She knew that he would ravage her, then kill her, then take all the horses. It would leave Patrick and the others exposed and unable to escape.

She lost all hope of saving herself, but tried to come up with a plan to give the others a chance. She knew that if Jens' got control of the horses, the others would be doomed. She decided that she had to free the horses. It might be hard for the men to find them again, but at least it gave them a chance. She knew if she frightened the horses their ties would come loose and they could escape. She looked past Jens, toward the horses. Wind was already acting nervous, eyes bulging while he stared at Jens with a look of pure hatred. He was pulling at the tether only slightly, stopping when he met the slight resistance of the rope. His training had taught him a lesson, that in this case, was the wrong lesson. She was going to have to do something to make him frightened enough to overcome his training.

It was certain that Jens would capture her, but she hoped he could not do it before she had a chance to free the horses. Her plan required quickness and a lot of luck.

She took a deep breath and bolted out of the bushes like a frightened pheasant, flying toward the horses with her knife thrust out in front of her, screaming like a banshee. Jens saw her immediately and darted in her direction, but slowed noticeably after his initial jump, still hurting from his bullet wounds. As she ran by the campfire she grabbed the cool end of a burning brand. She waved it in the air as she ran at the horses, still emitting a shrill cry. She beat Jens to the horses and waved the fire brand in their faces while yanking up and down on the line strung between two trees, to which the horses were all tethered. All too soon Jens reached her and grabbed her by her hair. But he got to her a second too late and from the corner of her eye Josefina could see the horses fleeing in fear.

"That wasn't very smart now, was it," Jens hissed into Josefina's ear. "How are your friends going to ride away now?"

Josefina scalp was pained by Jens' rough grasp of her hair. She reached up and clawed at the offending hand, leaving bloody scrapes. He howled and punished her for the scratches by cuffing her across her cheek with his free hand. Then he pulled down savagely on her hank of hair, forcing her to the ground. As she lay pinned to the dirt he pulled a pistol from his jacket pocket and pushed the point of the barrel roughly to her cheek.

"Try that again and I will blow your pretty face right off," he warned her. She could smell whiskey on his breath, a faint perfume fragrance mixed with it. She had no illusions about her situation. It was dire. Jens was not a man who knew any measure of mercy.

# CHAPTER SIXTY EIGHT

*WITHOUT A WORD OF EXPLANATION* I ran out of Jens' room and leaped down the stairs four at a time. I could hear the plodding boots of the others right behind me. Pa heard me coming and was on his feet, poised for action. I explained to him very briefly what had happened as I ran by him, headed for the exit.

Our little posse hit the dirt street running as fast as our boots could move. I heard some yelling behind me and I knew it was pa, trying to give some sort of instructions. But I was too blinded, and deafened, by my rage and my anger at myself for leaving Josefina alone in camp, to hear him. If I had calmed myself enough to listen to him I probably would have acted more soundly. But I didn't listen. I just plowed on ahead.

We were plenty winded by the time we approached camp. No one had caught up to me during the run. Probably because no one else was as motivated by anger and guilt as I was. Or maybe because they were not as in love as I was. But as crazy minded as I was, I at least had enough sense left to know I had to slow up and catch my breath before reaching the horse camp. It wouldn't do me, nor Josefina, any good if I showed up too winded to act.

I stopped running, slowing to a walk. Most of the others caught up to me quickly, all panting. But Riley lagged further behind, not yet well enough for a long run. We stopped to let him catch up to us.

"That was stupid," Pa said to me while we waited. I didn't reply. Pa stared at me for a few seconds, but nothing more was said by either of us. He turned away and walked back toward the struggling Riley. I watched him go, and in that exact moment I realized that Milksop was finally dead. Forever. It was a time I would remember distinctly for the rest of my life. What I recall most strongly about that moment was that I felt not one ounce of fear or uncertainty. My intentions were as clear as a cloudless sky, and my conviction to those intentions was absolutely unshakable. The opinions of others had no influence on me. I was my own man now, and I knew I would never go back.

"You stay here," I ordered Riley when he caught up with us. He looked me hard in the eyes. I looked back, even harder. And I knew what he was seeing in my gaze. He was seeing that there was no give in me. I meant what I said, no question. He nodded.

"All of you stay here," I told the others. "I don't need you, and I don't want you with me. What I do from here, I do on my own. It's the only way." I waited for someone to protest, but no one spoke. None of them liked it, especially Pa, but they all respected it.

Pa checked his gun to ensure that it was fully loaded and then handed it to me. "You'll need a backup weapon," he explained. I took the gun and put it in my belt. Pa stared at me for a second then nodded once and turned back. There was more said in that nod than a million words could ever express. It said that I was a man now.

# CHAPTER SIXTY NINE

*THE FIRST THING I NOTICED* when I walked into camp was that the horses were gone. I shuddered. Not at the thought of the missing horses, but at the thought of what I was going to do to Jens.

The camp fire was still burning brightly and I was having trouble seeing past it. I could see things clearly on the near side of it, but there was nothing there to see. No Josefina.

I moved slowly in a circle around the fire, ready for anything. I went the entire way around it, but still nothing. Still no Josefina. I waited, standing still and listening. Thinking. If she was gone, and the horses were gone, it meant Jens had her. I tried to think like Jens. Like the evil man he was. If I was him, would I stay in camp? Not if I had what I came here to get, Josefina. But where would he take her?

I examined the ground on the far side of the fire. The side furthest from town, he would not be taking her back there. He wouldn't want to take the chance that we were still there looking for him. There were so many tracks in the dirt, from our earlier visit, that it was hard to pick anything out. I walked to the outer edges of camp, where there were less tracks. I saw some leaves that were disturbed and a few broken twigs. I continued on, away from the camp, trying not to make any noise. I stopped every so often to listen, hoping to hear some signs of them.

The third time I stopped to listen, things were very quiet. Too quiet, not natural. I waited a little longer this time, wanting to figure out why there was a strange feeling in the air. A sudden crash in the brush behind me and a pounding of the earth startled me and I jumped back, tripping on a piece of sage. As I fell onto my back a mighty black monster leaped over my body. It shrieked an angry animal scream as it sped away, gone so fast I wondered if it was a ghost. It was no ghost though, it was real. It was Wind. I would recognize his voice anywhere. I could still hear the faint thuds of his pounding hooves, fading as he ran.

I laid in the dirt, stunned, and momentarily uncertain what action I should take next. I decided that getting up out of the dirt might be a good start. I dusted myself off and made up my mind what to do next. Trusting to Wind, I followed him. I went fast, no longer needing to attempt a silent approach. I ran in his wake for about five minutes, then heard his high whinny again, screaming into the night. I ran in the direction of his sounds. He must have stopped running because I could hear him more and more clearly as I gained on him.

I could tell by the sounds Wind was making that I was close, but it was still too dark to see things clearly. Then I saw a dark shadow, that was Wind, dashing around in a tight circle and rearing up on his hind legs occasionally. There were other motions around him but I couldn't make out what it was. I finally saw what it was when I was almost on top of them. It was Jens and Josefina. Jens had her by the hair and was dragging her around and around, trying to escape Wind.

Wind was in a wild fury and cut off any attempt Jens made to flee, as if he was pushing a stray calf back to the herd. When he could, he would run in on Jens and strike at him with his front hooves. I was worried that he might strike Josefina by mistake so I hollered at him to stop, at the same time taking aim with my pistol at Jens and praying for a clean shot at him. When Jens heard me holler he glanced past Wind for a second and saw me pointing my gun his way. He must have realized that Josefina had now become a liability for him and he dropped her and ran.

I ran to Josefina, praying that she was not harmed. Wind gave chase to Jens and after a few minutes I couldn't hear much from either of them. As badly as I wanted to kill Jens, I could not leave Josefina alone again. Once was bad enough.

"You OK?" I asked her, as I leaned over her, brushing the leaves and dirt from her hair. God she was pretty. I felt another strong pang of guilt for leaving her. I never should have listened to Pa and the others. I should have listened to my own gut, and heeded my own counsel.

"Jes, senor Patrick," she whispered. "I muy bueno now ju are here." I stroked her hair a little more and looked in her eyes. She smiled a little and I felt some relief.

"Can you stand up?" I asked her. She rubbed her scalp and then sat up. A minute later I helped her to her feet. She seemed steady on her feet, and I relaxed a little more.

"What did he do to you?"

"He yus pull my hair, and he hits my face one time too." She rubbed her cheek to make the point. We looked at each other not knowing what to say next. We were silent like that for about two minutes, then the the quiet of the night was shattered once again by the thunder of pounding horse hooves and the crash of their torsos against the brush and trees. A second later four men on horse back raced by us, only a few yards away.

"You stay here!" I heard Rowdy holler as he rode by. Then we heard all four of the riders laugh. They were on the heels of Wind, and Jens.

"What so funny?" Josefina asked.

"I'll tell you later."

I should have been sore as hell, for many reasons. I should have been sore that I didn't get to kill Jens in his room tonight, as planned. I should have been sore that the other men had come to help me instead of staying where I told them to stay. And I should have been real sore that they made fun of me as they rode by, hollering 'you stay here' as they rode off to kill Jens without me. So why was I smiling?

I'll tell you why I was smiling. The answer is easy. I was with Josefina again, and she was unharmed. Two very big reasons for me to smile. I walked her back to the camp and led her over to the fire and sat her on a warmed rock, making sure she was comfortable. Then I heated some water and made us some coffee. I handed her a cup of the coffee and then made us some broth from some jerky that I found in her saddle bags.

We sat by the fire for another thirty minutes without speaking. I watched her closely though. The coffee and broth seemed to help her, she was shaking less and even gave me a weak smile.

"You OK?" I asked her.

"Jes, much better," she said in a faint voice. "Thank ju for make me cafe and sopa."

"No problema," I said, surprised to hear myself using a Spanish word. It must have surprised Josefina as well. She turned toward me and smiled. Then she gave a short laugh, which raised my spirits a remarkable amount.

"Something wrong with my Spanish?" I asked her, knowing it was not the real reason that she laughed at me, but I wanted to keep the light mood going.

"Jes," she said seriously. "Mucho is wrong con ju Spanish." But she couldn't keep the straight face and broke out laughing. I laughed too, and we hugged each other while laughing like silly kids. But it didn't last long.

# CHAPTER SEVENTY

*JOSEFINA STOPPED LAUGHING* and pulled quickly away from me, looking off into the woods south of camp. A look of anxiety replaced her laughter and I peered in the same direction she was staring, trying to see what had frightened her. I saw nothing.

"What is it?" I asked her.

"Some caballos are coming. I hear them," she whispered. I listened closely for the sounds of horses, and within a few seconds I heard the faint thudding of horse hooves on the ground. I stood and grasped Josefina's hand.

"Come on," I told her as I pulled on her hand, leading her away from the firelight. We took cover behind a clump of bushes on the north side of the camp. Anyone approaching from the south would be unable to look directly beyond the fire without being blinded by it. It worked both ways though, we would be unable to see anything that came directly behind the fire from the south.

We heard the horses walk slowly into the camp. They were close enough to the fire for it to cast its light on them, but the fire blocked out a clear view of them. I wasn't going to give up our hidden location by moving so we stayed still and quiet, hoping they would come around the fire and reveal themselves. I didn't know exactly what I might do if they were foes, I knew only that I would do whatever it took to protect Josefina. Fortunately, they were not foes.

"Hello, the camp," I heard Pa holler. I breathed a sigh of relief, and I could feel a relaxation of Josefina's hand, which was still grasped in mine. We walked hand in hand from behind our bush.

"Howdy, Pa," I said clearly so he would know it was me. He walked his horse around the fire, following the direction of my voice.

"Is she OK?" he asked when he came into view of us.

"She'll be alright," I answered. "Bruised up a might, and shook up some."

"Thank God that's all the hurt she got. Jens could have done much worse," he sighed. The others had come around the fire and they all nodded their agreement. Rowdy was the last one in the line-up, and the back of his horse was still shielded by the fire so I could only see the front half of it.

"I got something for you," Rowdy said. He held up his right hand and I could see that he was holding a lead rope. It took me a second to realize that he also held his own horse's reins in his other hand. At first I couldn't fathom why he would have two leads on his horse, but then he pulled his right hand forward and I could see the nose of another horse come into view from behind Rowdy's mount. It was Wind.

I rushed to Winds side, dragging Josefina with me. I don't think she liked me doing that to her, but I wasn't about to let go of her for a while. Maybe quite a while. Wind nudged me a little and then rubbed his face on my forearm, his cue that he wanted me to scratch him under the chin. I obliged him. His eyelids lowered a little, like he was in heaven now. I felt the same way, in heaven. I was with the all the people who meant the most to me, especially Josefina, and Wind. At a moment like that, the last thing I wanted to think about was Jens. But I did think about him. I didn't want him barging in again and spoiling the mood. I looked around at the men, and they were all staring back at me, like they knew what was coming.

"Where is he?" I asked, a little venom in my tone that I thought I had not intended. But apparently I had. From the nods of the men I could tell it was the question they were expecting.

"He won't be bothering us any more," Kelly volunteered. I was surprised by the pleasure I heard in his voice when he said it. I didn't think he would ever cotton to the idea of being a vigilante.

"Who had the honors?" I asked.

"You did," Pa said, a hint of pride coming through in the statement.

"How is that possible?" I asked. "I saw him run off from here with my own eyes. He seemed in fair condition at the time too. And I never moved an inch from this here camp."

"You're right about that," Pa told me. "It wasn't exactly you who done it. Exactly," he said, looking confused.

"Which is it then?" I asked him. "I don't get it. Either I killed him or I didn't. And as far as I can tell I never touched a hair on him."

Pa stared at me blankly, unsure how to answer me. He looked around at Rowdy, Riley, and Kelly like he was hoping for some kind of help from them. Apparently they had no help to offer because all they did was shrug in response to Pa's silent plea. He looked back at me with a blank stare. After a second or two he spoke.

"It was your horse that done it," he blurted at me. "Good as you doin it yourself if you ask me," he tried explaining. I still didn't get it. I looked at Josefina with a questing look, wondering if it was only my ignorance that betrayed me or if maybe she didn't understand Pa any better than I did. The blank look on her face told me she was as clueless as I was.

"Sorry, Pa. But you aren't making much sense. Are you telling me that Wind had something to do with this?"

"I'm telling you he had everything to do with it," Pa said. "By the time we caught up with Jens, Wind had him under control."

"I'm tellin ya, Patrick, it was a sight to see," Riley volunteered. "I'm glad I seen it once in my life, but at the same time I hope I never have to see it again."

"Amen to that," Rowdy agreed. "Unless another Jens comes along. I don't think I would mind so much witnessin it again if it was Jens, or someone equally as evil."

"Will one of you just tell us what happened?" I begged. "Please."

"May not be something for a lady to hear," Pa said, nodding at Josefina.

"She was ready to cut out Jens' heart with her Arkansas toothpick," I informed him. "Was it worse than that?"

"I reckon not."

"Then tell us what happened. Please."

"When we caught up to them, Wind had Jens pinned against a tree," Pa started. "When Jens would try to go around the tree to escape, Wind was there ahead of him. I never seen such speed and agility."

"You ain't lyin, Shawn," Riley agreed. "That is one hell of a horse. Much more than we thought he was when you took him, Patrick. And we thought he was the best in the country at the time."

"Anyway," Pa continued, "Jens had nowhere to go, and just when we were trying to get Wind to back off, so's we could shoot Jens, he blocked our approach. It was like he wanted to keep us away from Jens. We hollered at him and tried to get hold of him, but he was plumb crazed. The look in his eyes made me shiver.

"We tried and tried to get him off Jens, but nothing worked. Then all of a sudden Wind struck. He went on his hinds and he just pummeled and pummeled, over and over, with his front legs. They were movin so fast that they were a blur. Within ten seconds he must have clubbed Jens a hundred times with his hooves. 'Course the last ninety eight of them Jens was already on the ground, a bloody mess."

"Yeah, it was pretty awful," Kelly agreed. "But we had no idea how to stop Wind. We  had to stand and watch as he turned Jens into a pile of mush. Never seen nothing so horrible."

"It was amazing," Rowdy said with pride. There was a hint of a smile on his face for an instant. Then it was replaced with a sheepish look, like he'd made a mistake and done something wrong. He looked around at us, hoping  we hadn't noticed. But we did. I also noticed a slight grin on all their faces. But it was Josefina who first mentioned something about it.

"Ju no looks very sorry," she observed. The grins on the faces of the men grew wide. Then Pa laughed a short snort of a chuckle before controlling himself. But it was too late, the others burst out in laughter.

"Sorry," Pa said, still trying to stifle his laughing. "But, well, I can't think of a better end for the asshole. It was a wonderful thing to watch him go that way." He snickered again and again until Josefina laughed. Seeing her happiness filled my heart and I laughed too. We all laughed for a good few minutes, then we sighed.

"Did you bury him?" I asked.

"I would kill the first man who tried to bury that son of a bitch," Riley said. He said it in such a menacing way that I truly feared for any man who crossed him.

I guess Josefina agreed with Riley's assessment. "Let the animals eat his carcass and spread his bones across the world," she said.

"Amen," Kelly and Rowdy said.

# CHAPTER SEVENTY ONE

*WE FED AND WATERED THE HORSES,* then tethered them to a newly made tree line. I, however, kept Wind by my side. I just couldn't bring myself to separate from him. He didn't seem to mind, since I was constantly scratching under his chin.

We sat around the camp fire after eating a meal and drank some coffee. We re-hashed the days events for a couple of hours until most of us became sleepy. Josefina and I crawled into our bedroll, but I had a hard time going to sleep. Sometime around midnight I crawled out of the sack and grabbed a cup of lukewarm coffee. I wandered the camp, checking on the horses. Wind followed along like a puppy.

Almost unconsciously I reached for the gun in my belt, but it wasn't there. I wondered why I was reaching for it, what made me do it. It was an uneasiness, a growing certainty that I might need it, but I could not think of why. I went back to my bedroll and retrieved my gun belt from beside it. I put the belt on, ensuring it was properly tied around my waist, then I found myself walking away from camp, towards town. I moved slowly, quietly, glad that Wind had decided to stay with the other horses. I hadn't gone far when I had a bad feeling. I pulled my gun and cocked it.

I stood still, listening. After a few minutes passed I heard a sound. It was a quiet snap of a small twig. I stood motionless. A minute later I heard another twig snap, closer this time. Then I heard whispered voices.

"I smell horse shit," the whisper said.

"Yeah, we're close," the other whisper said.

"What do we do if Jens is not there?" the other whisper asked.

"He's here."

I waited, knowing they they were  getting closer. When they were within a few yards of me I spoke.

"You are too late," I said, breaking the silence.

I was ready for their reaction and jumped to my right after I spoke. They threw down as I expected, but I was a jump ahead of them and I let loose with my pistol, firing all six shots. Both men went down. I laid on the ground for a few seconds to see if they would get up again, but there was no motion. I walked over to them and kicked their bodies. They didn't move or react to my kick. They couldn't, they were too dead.

I recognized them as a couple of Jens' gang. The first people I had ever killed. I had no regret of the fact. I had no emotion at all, unless it was satisfaction. I was satisfied that I had rid the world of evil men. And in that moment, I realized I was capable of killing without regret. I thought of Riley, and of how much I had become like him. Riley who I hated months ago when he gave me Wind. Riley who I now loved. Who was I now? A killer? I had just killed two men, so I guess I was a killer. So was I bad? Was I a bad man? I was not sure about the answers to those questions. But I was sure about one thing. I was not the man who left Richmond. I was not Milksop McGee. Milksop was, in fact, such a distant memory that it was difficult for me to even imagine that I had once been him.

The gunfire had woken up the others in camp. Pa walked up beside me as I was staring at the dead men on the ground.

"It's a shock," he said to me. "The first time is always a shock. Worse than a shock. It will haunt you forever. I won't sugar coat it for you, son. But if you think about it, you were not given a choice. People like Jens, they have a choice, and he chose to murder people who did not deserve it. They do it for other reasons than self preservation. They do it for pleasure. Never believe that you are like them. You will lose sleep over this killing for the rest of your life because you are a good man. People like Jens, and the men you just killed, would never lose sleep over killing. In fact they would take a perverse pleasure in it. They are flawed. You are not, so therefore you will suffer. Its the way the world is, son."

I walked away without responding. There was nothing I could say, so I went to Josefina. I hugged her and she silently led me back to our sleeping bag, where I lay awake the remainder of the night. I was vaguely aware that Riley and Pa stood guard for the night.

In the early morning, before the gray dawn, we were all awake and having coffee around the fire. No one spoke. But in the silence many thoughts were echoed. All of us had endured a common experience. All of us now felt a common emotion from having done so. We were one, in at least this one experience. And without saying so, we knew that a verbal discussion would diminish the impact of the experience. We must have instinctively understood that a discussion would somehow create a little bit of a separation between us. And it must have been true that none of us wanted to experience any amount of separation.

# CHAPTER SEVENTY TWO

*BREAKING CAMP THAT DAY WAS EMOTIONAL.* Pa and Riley were going to Kansas City to catch a train home. Kelly was headed back to his home to check in with his boss. Rowdy planned to go to Antonio's ranch in Texas to see if he could revive the herd and make a go of it again. That left me and Josefina.

Me and Josefina hugged Pa and Riley with teary eyes and promised to see them again in the future.

"Maybe you will come back to Richmond some day," Pa suggested.

"Maybe," I answered. Pa nodded. He knew I wasn't ready for that town yet.

"But you will call for me if you need me?"

"Yes, Pa."

I shook Riley's hand. "I will never be able to repay you for Wind you know," I said to him.

"You already have, Patrick," he said. "The minute Wind killed Jens your debt was paid." I nodded in understanding.

"Thanks," I said. Pa and Riley rode off toward town, leaving Kelly and Rowdy still in camp with us. I was about to give my heartfelts to Kelly, but he swung up in his saddle, rode off and waved a goodbye, without a word. I waved back, even though he had his back to us already and wouldn't see it. I understood his reason for the silent departure. He didn't like goodbyes, and I didn't blame him.

"Ain't much of a talker is he?" Rowdy said. His question turned my eyes from the receding Kelly and I looked over at him.

"Reckon not," I said. Josefina was in my arms now, and I appreciated her timing more than ever. She saved me from an embarrassing tear-eyed moment. I wondered, again, if she really could read my mind.

"I'd like you both to come help me start a new heard," Rowdy said. I glanced at Josefina for a second. In that look, in that second, we made silent a pact. We were going back to the Miracle Valley, the one that Rowdy showed us, to start our own operation.

"I think we got our own plans in mind, Rowdy," I said. "But I'm sure we will meet on the trail. And if you ever need us, you come askin. We'll come runnin. You'll find us in Miracle Basin." Rowdy smiled a knowing smile, kinda smug. Like he expected my answer already.

"Thought so," he said. "But first tell me where the heck Miracle Basin is. I never heard of it."

"Maybe you never heard the name," I said. "But you was the one who showed it to us. Its what we named that hidden valley that you all wandered into by accident with Antonio."

"Good name for it," Rowdy replied. "And anytime you ask me for help, I'll come runnin too."

"Thanks, Rowdy." We shook hands and he rode out just like Kelly did, with a wave.

Josefina and I stared after Rowdy for many minutes, until he disappeared from sight. Partly I stared at his back because I didn't trust myself to not cry. Like I said already, I think Josefina can read my mind because she didn't move until I did. I turned to her and looked deep into her eyes.

"Senorita," I said. "Shall we go?"

"I no like that word," she said.

"You mean you want to stay?" I asked.

"No, I mean I no like the word Senorita."

"Oh," I said. I stalled a few seconds, pretending to myself that I didn't know what it was she was inferring. But the more I considered it, the more I didn't really want to avoid the bare truth of what she was saying. In fact I kinda liked the idea.

"Senora," I said. "Shall we go?"

"Senora Que?"

"Senora McGee," I said. "Shall we go?" She smiled. She beamed. I beamed. I'd finally got it right. 'Course I knew we weren't bona fide husband and wife yet, but it made my intentions clear. And that was what she wanted to know.

## PART SEVEN – HAPPILY EVER AFTER

Happiness is not just a feeling.
Its a whole dang passel of em.

# CHAPTER SEVENTY THREE

*OUR FIRST STOP WAS MIRACLE BASIN.* As we had hoped, it was just as we had left it. No one else had discovered it in our absence. We spent one night there and the next morning we hit the trail.

We were some kind of anxious to get hitched, as the saying goes. Josefina led the way to a small village of mostly Spanish people a couple of days ride south. The village had a priest, which was an important part of choosing to ride there.

If you got a lick of sense you can guess what happened in the village after we arrived. But what you might not guess, and I surely didn't, was that the entire village came out for our wedding and it became a fantastic fandango. And that was mostly because it was where Josefina's parents and family lived. Another thing I never would have guessed.

We stayed in the village for a week after the wedding. It was very nice, being with the family and doing a lot of nothing. But the doing nothing part got to me. It seems that being around the family made Josefina uncomfortable doin the thing that married couples are allowed to do after bein married, if you know what I mean. Which made me uncomfortable, if you know what I mean.

So after a week we headed back to Miracle Basin, which was kinda where it all started between us. At least in the physical sense. You may recall the small cabin. And the absence of the others in our party at the time. I sure do recall it. Vividly.

After returning to Miracle Basin we consummated our wedding, consummating being a new word to me. I don't mind telling you that I like the word.

The morning after consummation, we began building the Miracle Basin Beef and Cattle Company.

# CHAPTER SEVENTY FOUR

*A YEAR AFTER OUR CONSUMMATION IN MIRACLE BASIN* we had our first herd ready for the drive to the Wichita stock market. We set out at three in the morning, a few hours before daylight on a clear, late spring day. Our modest herd consisted of only twenty heifers. Nothing to write home about, but it was only our first year. We needed the sale, no matter how small, to build up the size of the herd for next season.

We were nearly upon the cutoff to the hidden little valley where I had been shot by Jens. I was lost in the memory of the spot, and not paying close attention to my surroundings, so I was surprised when I finally heard horse hooves very close by. Two men were riding hell bent toward us and evil was evident in their eyes. For a split second I realized how easy it had become for me to recognize evil in a man. But after that split second I was all action, no more thinking. I cleared leather and fired two shots so quickly that it took me a second to realize I'd done it. By that time two men were on the ground, and those two men were dead. My bullets had caught them both in the heart. I recognized them as two more of Jens' gang. I wondered how many of them were left, and for how long would they be gunnin for me.

Without a glance back at the two dead men I turned to Josefina and said, "Shall we ride on in to town, Senora?" She didn't answer and I rode on ahead toward Wichita. Josefina fell in next to me but didn't speak, but she did glance at me every once in a while though. I wondered what she was thinking, but was afraid to ask her. After about a half mile of riding she finally spoke.

"Ju haf become bery hard mans, senor Patrick," she said softly. I didn't answer right away, considering what she said. I could see why she thought the way she did, especially after she'd witnessed the way I had just dispatched the two men who attacked us. And in a way she was right, I had become a hard man. But in my own estimation, what really counted for something, was that I had become a man. I didn't think I could ever kill for the mere pleasure of it. But I also knew that I could never stand by and let evil men kill decent people. People I loved, like Josefina.

"Are you afraid of me?" I asked her. She took a minute to answer, which worried me.

"Should I be?" she asked in return.

"The only people who need fear me are those who threaten the people I love, like you, or Pa, or Riley, or Rowdy."

"Or Wind?"

"Yes, or Wind," I said with a smile. She smiled back, and I could breathe again.

Wind nickered.

# EPILOGUE

*WE GOT LUCKY AT THE STOCKYARD IN WICHITA.* Seems there was a shortage of beef in the country at the time, and meat prices were soaring. We made twice the expected profit. That meant that we could double the next seasons herd. We left town with a new freight wagon and team, loaded with supplies. I was relieved to be going. I had been constantly looking over my shoulder for more of Jens' men, but never saw any. I hoped that meant that they were finished, but how could I be sure.

Two hours down the trail back to Miracle Valley we stopped at the unmarked cutoff up over the rise and into the hole I had tried to hide in, before Jens found me and shot me.

Without speaking I reined Wind off the trail and rode up to the top of the Ridge. Josefina brought the wagon up behind us and gave me a knowing look. And the rest, as the saying goes, is history.

CLIFF BONNERS FACEBOOK PAGE:
facebook.com/CBonnerauthor.

TOUGH CHOICES- A mystery novel by Cliff Bonner
Also available on Amazon or Barnes and Noble

Made in the USA
Las Vegas, NV
13 October 2023

78609182R00116